The **KAYAK**

The
KAYAK

DEBBIE SPRING

thistledown press

Thistledown Press Ltd.
633 Main Street
Saskatoon, Saskatchewan, S7H oJ8
www.thistledownpress.com

Library and Archives Canada Cataloguing in Publication
Spring, Debbie, 1953-
The kayak / Debbie Spring.

ISBN 978-1-897235-71-3

I. Title.
PS8587.P734K39 2010 jC813'.6 C2010-900917-7

Cover photograph©istockphoto.com
Cover and book design by Jackie Forrie
Printed and bound in Canada

 Canada Council   Conseil des Arts
for the Arts   du Canada

 Canadian   Patrimoine
Heritage   canadien

We acknowledge the support of the Canada Council for the Arts, the
Saskatchewan Arts Board, and the Government of Canada through the Book
Publishing Industry Development Program for our publishing program.

ACKNOWLEDGEMENTS

For my loving family; Morris, Sandy, Cynthia, Judy, Miriam, Oren, Jasmine, Elan, Patricia, Josh, Mandy, Betty and Gerry. A special thank you Fred, for your insights and constant support.

Many thanks to Thistledown Press for believing in me and for the editorial guidance of R.P. MacIntyre.

1

THE CHOPPY WAVES RISE AND FALL. My kayak bobs like a cork in the swirling waters of Georgian Bay. I love it. I feel wild and free. The wind blows my hair into my eyes. I concentrate on balance. I stop stroking with my double-bladed paddle and push my bangs back.

This is my special place. Out here, I feel safe and secure. My parents watch from the shore even though I wear my life jacket and emergency whistle. I am one with the kayak. The blue boat is an extension of my legs. I can do anything; I can go anywhere. Totally independent. Totally in control of my life. It's so different back at shore.

I approach Cousin Island, where I have to steer around the submerged rocks. In the shallows, a school of largemouth bass darts between the weeds. A wave pushes me towards the rocks. I push off with my paddle and I head out towards the middle of Kilcoursie Bay, where powerful swirls of wind and current toss me about.

The clouds move in, warning signs. I turn the kayak and head back to my point of departure. The waves peak wildly as the storm threatens. My arms ache.

I don't want to go back to shore. My parents treat me the same now as when I was a child, not wanting to admit that I'm seventeen and grown-up.

Just off my bow, a loon preens its black mottled feathers. I stare at its white throated necklace. It sounds its piercing cry and disappears under the water. I hold my breath, waiting for it to resurface. Time slows. Finally, the loon reappears in the distance. I exhale.

I notice a windsurfer with a flashy neon green and purple sail gaining on me. My stomach does flip flops as he races, dangerously close. "Look out," I yell. I quickly steer out of the way. He just misses me. *Stupid kid, he's not even wearing a life jacket.* I shake my head. The boy is out of control. He's heading straight for the rocks at Cousin Island. "Drop the sail!" I call.

He does and not a second too soon. He just misses a jagged rock. I slice through the waves and grab onto his white surfboard.

"Can you get back to shore?" I ask.

"I don't know what I'm doing." His voice trembles. Is it from the cold?

The windsurfer looks about my age. I glance at his tanned muscles and sandy, blond hair. He seems vulnerable and afraid. His blue eyes narrow. "Now what?" he asks.

I reach into the cockpit and take out a rope. "Hold on." I toss the rope. He misses. I throw it again and he catches it. "Paddle to the back of my kayak with your hands." His board moves directly behind me. "Tie the other end through that yellow loop." I point. He fumbles for what seems like several painful minutes. "Got it."

I stroke hard, straining to move us.

"Hit it," the boy calls.

"What?"

"That's what you shout, in water skiing when you're ready to take off."

I smile. Slowly, we make our way. My paddle dips into the water, first to the right, then to the left. Beads of sweat form on my forehead. Suddenly, I surge ahead. I turn around. "You let go." I circle and give him back the rope. "Wrap it around your wrist."

"Sorry."

"It's okay. What's your name?"

"Jamie." His teeth chatter. The water churns around his board. He is soaked. I don't like the blue colour of his lips.

"I'm Teresa. Don't worry, Jamie. It will be slow because we're going against the current but I promise to get you back in one piece." It takes too much energy to talk and paddle. Instead, I get him chatting. "Tell me about yourself."

"I thought I was good at all water sports, but windsurfing sure isn't one of them," he laughs.

I don't mean to answer. It just comes out. "Maybe with practice."

"Dumb to go out so far. I don't know what I'm doing." He changes the rope to the other hand, flexing the stiff one.

The wind changes. A big wave hits Jamie sideways, knocking him into the dark, chilly water, trapping him underneath the sail.

"Jamie!" I scream. The wind swallows my voice.

2

JAMIE IS THRASHING ABOUT TRAPPED BENEATH the sail like a fish flapping on the bottom of a fishing boat. The fabric rises and falls. My heart races as his motions get weaker. I have to do something fast.

Quickly, I position my boat perpendicular to his board, making a T. I drop my paddle, grabbing the tip of his sail at the mast. I tug. Nothing. The water on top of the sail makes it heavy. I drop it. I try again. One, two, three, heave. I grunt, as I break the air pocket and lift the sail a couple of inches. It's enough to let Jamie wriggle out. He explodes to the surface, gulping in air, then pulls himself safely onto the surfboard. I reach over to help untangle the rope from around his foot. I can see an ugly rope burn. His body is shaking.

My kayak starts to tip. I throw my weight to the opposite side to keep from flipping. "Keep hold of the rope."

"Got it."

"Where's my paddle?" My throat tightens. I search the water. "There it is," I sigh with relief. It's floating a few feet away. I pull through the water, reach out and grab the shaft.

"Hang on, Jamie." The current changes and we ride the swelling waves like a bucking bronco.

I have to keep away from shore or the waves will smash us against the granite. Just as we clear the rocks, a cross-current hits me. My kayak flips. I'm sitting upside down in the water. *Don't panic. Do the Eskimo roll.* I get my paddle in the ready position. Then I swing the blade away from the boat's side. I arch my back around and through, keeping my head low. I sweep my blade through the water, pulling hard. I right the kayak and gasp for air.

"You gave me a heart attack." Jamie looks white.

"Caught me by surprise." We drift, while I catch my breath. The clouds turn black. The water calms. "For now, it will be easy going. It's going to storm any minute." I paddle fast and hard as the rain comes down in buckets.

"I'm already wet, so it doesn't matter," Jamie jokes.

I like his sense of humour, but I'm out of practise talking to a guy. I haven't had a boyfriend in a long time and the guys at school, ignore me.

"I feel so helpless," Jamie says.

He feels helpless? What about me?

The kayak drifts. I see my parents anxiously waiting for me on shore.

The Kayak

My father runs into the water to help. Everything happens real fast when he takes control. Before I know it, Jamie and I are safely back on shore. My mother runs over with towels. Jamie wraps the towel around him and pulls the windsurfer onto the sand. I stay in my kayak. Half the kayak is on land. The rest is in the water. I feel trapped, like a beached whale.

Jamie comes back and stands over me. "Do you need help?" he asks.

I shake my head, no. *Go away!* I scream in my head. *Go away, everybody!*

"Thanks for saving my skin," Jamie says.

"Next time, wear a life jacket."

Jamie doesn't flinch. "You're right. That was dumb." It is pouring even harder. Jamie hugs the wet towel around him. "Aren't you getting out?" he asks.

"Yes," but I don't move. Jamie gets a funny look on his face when he sees my mother waiting with the empty wheelchair.

"Say something." My voice quivers. A fat bullfrog croaks and jumps into the water. I want to jump in after him and swim away somewhere safe. I say nothing more.

"Teresa," he clears his throat. "I didn't know."

I watch his discomfort. I've seen it all before. Awkwardness. Forced conversation. A feeble excuse and a fast get-away. My closer friends tried a little harder.

They lasted two or three visits. Then, they stopped coming around.

The silence drags on as my father lifts me from my kayak and helps me into my wheelchair. A mosquito buzzes around my head. So annoying. Why can't the bug and Jamie both leave? It lands on my arm and I smack it.

"Do you like roasting marshmallows?" asks Jamie.

"Huh?"

"I like mine burnt to a crisp."

I hate small talk. My hands turn white, as I clutch the armrests of my wheelchair. "What you really want to know is how long I've been crippled."

Jamie winces. He doesn't say anything. I wish he would leave. The air feels heavy and suffocating. I decide to make it easy for him. I'll go first. I push on the wheels with my hands. The sand is wet. The wheels bury, instead of thrusting the wheelchair forward. I stop pushing. Another helpless moment. My parents are watching, waiting for my signal to look after me.

Jamie puts his hand on my shoulder. "Would you like to join me and my friends at a campfire tonight? I need a date. Everybody is a couple, except me. Where's your campsite?"

"Granite Saddle number 1026." *Why do I tell him? What's the matter with me?* I stare at my wheelchair and then at my kayak — two images of me: the helpless child on land and the independent woman on water. I blink and the land and water merge. I become one.

I smile back at him.

Jamie pushes me past my parents who stare at me, in confusion. "It's okay. I'll take Teresa to your campsite." My parents walk behind at a safe distance, moving slowly, despite the rain. We stop at my tent. I smell the fragrance of wet pine needles.

"I'll pick you up at nine." An ember flickers in the wet fireplace, catching our eyes. Sparks rise up into the sky. Jamie takes my hand. "One other thing."

"Yes?"

"Bring the marshmallows."

3

I WHEEL MYSELF UP TO OUR BIG, blue, eight-person tent. Eight people would have to be packed like sardines to fit in this tent. I feel that it's crowded just with the four of us. For years, we've camped here for our holidays because Georgian Bay has the best waves for kayaking and so many islands to explore. My parents love the country and my sister Karen loves swimming and playing in the waves. What twelve-year-old wouldn't? The only difference is we now have the handicapped campsite, wheelchair accessible and close to the main washroom. The downside is that we are up the hill and too far for me to come and go from the beach on my own.

Kayaking is the only thing keeping me sane and my parents know that. The shrink suggested that we take a month here, to get me doing things again. Back home, I kind of lost interest in life. Not that I tried to do anything stupid like committing suicide, it's just that I didn't feel up to doing much or going anywhere. I felt tired all of the time. All the energy seemed sucked right out of me like a vampire had bitten me. Kayaking makes me feel alive. I don't ever want to leave here. What do I have to look forward to back in the city? Hours of TV?

I peek in through the window. Karen is sprawled out on top of my black sleeping bag reading a Spiderman comic. "Help me get into the tent," I call. She reluctantly gets up.

Karen tilts my wheelchair on its back wheels further than she needs to, making me feel like I'm going to fall backwards. She does that to get back at me for bugging her as she pushes me over the lip. The tent zips up the middle, dividing it into two equal rooms. Karen and I have the front portion. Last year, before the accident, my parents had the front, but it's easier this way.

Karen flops herself down, lying on a diagonal. "Shove over," I say. I take my towel from my wheelchair bag and spread it out over my sleeping bag so I don't wet it with my bathing suit. I lower myself down. Underneath the bag is an air mattress to cushion the hard ground. "Brr, I'm soaked." It takes me a long time to undress and change. "Where's my brush?"

"Here." Karen takes it from her pile and tosses it over.

I pull out a big brown fur ball from my brush, Karen's hair. I know it's hers because I have chestnut hair. I get the red highlights from my father who used to have red hair, but now he's bald. "I hate when you take my stuff without asking."

Karen shrugs then scratches. "I have so many mosquitoes bites."

"I can't tell if they're bites or freckles."

"Very funny." A mosquito lands on her arm and she squishes it. "Gross, blood, *my* blood and you let it in."

Through the screen window, I can see Mom and Dad busy hanging up wet clothes on the clothesline under the orange tarp. They're always working, even on vacation. I used to help, but now all I am to them is a burden. The wind swings the clothes, back and forth. A red squirrel chatters and chases a black squirrel away. It is territorial. I am too. I hate it when my parents come into my room at home without knocking. My room is my space. My parents used to respect that, but now they constantly invade my privacy.

I look in the hand mirror and brush my wet hair. "What am I going to do with this rug?" I tug at the tangles. My fingers are all thumbs as I try to braid my hair. I throw my brush down in frustration.

"Who's gonna see you anyway?" Karen blows a bubble with her gum.

"Thanks a lot." Karen has many irritating habits. She also bites her nails. "You look like a cow chewing its cud."

"Sor-ry." Crack goes her gum.

"For your information, I'm going out tonight." Now I have Karen's full attention.

"Where are we going?"

"Not we, me," I correct.

"Mom," Karen whines. "Why can't I go with Teresa?"

Mom peeks in through the side window. "What are you talking about?"

"Teresa says she's going out and I'm not."

"Teresa, what's this all about?"

"Jamie invited me to a campfire tonight."

Mom raises her eyebrows. She is about to ask me a million questions, but Karen beats her to it.

"Who's Jamie?" Karen asks. She looks from Mom to Dad, back to me. It's killing her that she doesn't know. I pause to make her squirm.

"This guy I rescued on a windsurfer."

"No, way," says Karen.

"Yes, way. Why can't the princess save the knight? Welcome to the twenty-first century."

"Teresa has a boyfriend, Teresa has a boyfriend," chants Karen.

"Shut up." I throw a pillow at her. She ducks and sticks out her tongue.

"It will be cancelled because of the rain," Karen blurts out.

I stiffen as the lightning flashes and lights up the sky. The thunder claps so loudly that I jump. Karen's right.

It might get cancelled unless it clears up. I have mixed feelings. I want to go, but what if his friends don't like me? What if Jamie asked me because he thinks that he owes me? A heaviness engulfs me and I just want to sleep.

My mind wanders. It has been almost a full year, but it seems like a lifetime ago that I used to have lots of friends. Since the accident, we seem to have nothing in common. I still get the token invitation, but I don't really fit in.

Before, I belonged to the track team. Running cleared my mind. I was fast. My team nicknamed me 'Bullet'. It helped that I had long legs allowing me a long stride. I ran the last leg of the team relay. I loved the competitive spirit, the companionship and winning trophies, ribbons, and medals.

I used to jog together with my boyfriend, Rick. We'd run in the woods and sometimes he'd steal a kiss. If the running didn't increase my heartbeat, his kisses sure did. Now he's found another girl to run with and kiss.

Mom pokes her head in. "Do you need anything?"

"I'm okay."

"You sure?"

"I'm fine."

"Call if you need me." Mom goes back out in the rain and I hear her opening and closing the van, putting things away, always the busy bee.

The Kayak

I miss my old life when I used to come and go as I pleased. Now I need my mother to take me everywhere. It's humiliating. Suffocating.

Mom looks tired all the time. She stopped working and going out with her friends, all to look after me. Poor Mom.

Both of my parents have sacrificed so much for me. They spent their life savings to renovate the house to make it wheelchair accessible — from ramps, to wider doorways, a low bathtub with bars and a seat elevator for the stairs.

They had promised Karen that she could renovate her room. She was so excited when she picked out all the colours, and other changes that she wanted. But the expense of making our home wheelchair accessible ended up way higher than expected and they ran out of money. Karen always gets the short end of the stick. It's a wonder that she doesn't hate me.

Tonight the fire pit is soaked and the wood won't catch so Dad starts the Coleman stove. Most people out here use their barbeques to cook all of their meals, but since I like the taste better, Dad humours me and usually cooks over an open fire.

"Nothing exotic, hotdogs for us and veggie hot dogs for Teresa," Mom announces.

Karen groans, "Not again."

I don't care. My stomach is too tied up in knots to eat. Being stuck in a wheelchair, I have to watch my calories. It helps that I'm vegetarian. Ever since I was seven and learned where meat came from, I stopped eating it. I love animals too much. But my parents serve me fish once in a while because they worry I'm not getting enough protein.

I took up wheelchair basketball because I needed to burn calories. It also kept my parents and doctor off my case to get a social life. They all thought I was such a great sport, but I was only doing it so I didn't turn into a blob of fat. I don't have to worry about getting fat while camping because I do so much swimming and kayaking. I certainly don't miss playing basketball. I'm not really into team sports.

I wonder if my parents are wishing the rain keeps up so that I don't go out with a boy they don't know. I'm hoping that the rain keeps up too and the campfire is cancelled. I mean who in their right mind would want to go out with a cripple?

It stops raining.

4

For the next hour, the rain starts and stops, a real tease.

By eight-thirty, I'm climbing the walls. There's no way he can call to tell me about a change in plans. Karen checks to see if the drops of water are coming from the overhanging trees or if it started to rain again.

I wait stiffly.

"Just spitting," Karen reports. "You gonna chicken out if it stops?"

"No way. I want to go," I lie. I get ready just in case.

But precisely at nine, Jamie shows up. I like a guy who's on time. "Thought the marshmallow roast might be cancelled because of the rain." I clasp my shaking fingers tightly in my lap.

"Never. We found a secluded place that's really sheltered. Got the marshmallows?"

"Right here." I point to the bag attached to my chair.

"Let's go."

"Sounds good to me."

"Ah, do I push you, or what?"

"Only if my wheels get stuck."

"Cool."

We head out. Neither of us talk. I don't know what to say and neither does he. The air is tense and damp. I wonder if this is a thank-you date or a pity date?

All the campsites we pass are bustling with activity. Kids are running around like maniacs. Parents look ready to pull their own hair out. Rainy days are hard on everybody. The smell of hamburgers, chicken and hot dogs fills my nose and my stomach rumbles. It's a reminder that I didn't eat much for dinner. I hope Jamie didn't hear it or I'd die of embarrassment.

"So, how long you camping here?" he asks.

I jump. At least he's finally talking. "A couple more weeks and you?"

"Me too. Same as most my friends."

"What are they like?" I ask.

"Wild and crazy, like you."

Like me? I can't believe he said that. How can I be wild and crazy rolling along in my specialty wheelchair?

"I've never seen a wheelchair like yours," says Jamie.

"This is an all-terrain wheelchair. I can take it on gravel, grass, into the water and through sand. The extra–wide, all-terrain wheels are especially good for uneven ground."

"I get it," says Jamie. "It's like a mountain bike is better for off road."

"Right."

"Why didn't you get a power model?" he asks.

"You have to be rich to afford one of those. They cost around ten-thousand dollars."

Jamie whistles.

"I prefer the exercise," I say. I love this wheelchair, but it's not perfect. Sometimes my wheels get stuck." And one of those times has to be now. I let out a groan in frustration. "Can you give me a hand?" I ask.

"No prob." Jamie pushes me so hard that my wheelchair tips forward and I go flying out and land sprawled out in a puddle. Jamie looks stunned but when he sees I'm not hurt, breaks out laughing.

I stare at him in disbelief. "Aren't you going to help me up?"

"Sor . . ." he has another laughing fit. "Can I take your picture?"

"You've got to be kidding."

"I'm studying photography and graphic arts at University of Ottawa. I would love to have a photo portfolio of you. I can see it now, 'Disabled girl; nothing throws her. Unstoppable'."

"I want to see them first!"

"Great!" He snaps away. Finally, he lifts me under the arms, grunting as he puts me back in my chair.

"I guess you don't know your own strength." I can't help smiling. "Can I see them now?"

"Only if you don't slug me."

He shows me the pictures of me sprawled out in the mud. I have half a mind to delete them. But then, I look at it objectively. "It really captures the moment." I smile.

"Do you want to go back and change?"

"No, I want to make a big splash with your buddies."

This gets him started again. The laughing is contagious and I join in. "Teresa, I like your sense of humour."

"I'd call yours slapstick or slap-sick," I say.

He smiles. "Seems like whenever I see you you're soaking wet."

"Very funny."

We get to the day-use picnic area where the fire pits and picnic tables are under a roof.

"This is your secret place?" I mock. "Everybody knows about it."

"It's dry isn't it?"

"Jamie, over here." A muscular, short guy with dark hair waves.

"Pasquali," Jamie shouts back.

I face a group of kids, some smoking and some drinking beer. All of a sudden I feel very embarrassed that my clothes are soaked and splattered with mud.

"Who's your date?" a well-endowed girl asks.

The Kayak

"Kat, I'd like you to meet, Teresa. She taught me about the finer art of windsurfing." He winks at me.

"Really?" she says in a sarcastic tone staring at my wheelchair.

A broad-shouldered boy puts his arm around her and she shrugs him off. "Not now, Bruno." He frowns and joins the other guys playing hacky sack.

The next few minutes are a blur of names and faces being introduced to me. Everybody seems friendly enough, except Kat. What's her problem?

Jamie is busy snapping pictures, but he seems to be focussed a lot on Kat. Is it because she's so drop dead gorgeous, or is it because she's an interesting subject?

"Why don't we all go horseback riding tomorrow?" Kat asks. She gives me a sweet smile though her eyes are cold.

Then I see it.

Kat is suddenly all over Bruno, but it's a display for Jamie who can't keep his eyes off her. Is Jamie's just using me to get back at her for something?

I want nothing to do with it.

Everybody agrees what a great idea horseback riding is. Jamie looks at me apologetically. My stomach feels all in knots. "Go, Jamie. Don't think twice about it because I'm a water person." He hesitates. "It's fine, really," I insist.

"Really? See you after riding then? Maybe go for a swim?"

"I'll be pretty waterlogged by then."

"Is this a brush off?" Jamie frowns.

"Of course not," I lie.

"Better not be."

I change the subject with a shiver. "I'm chilled right through. Could you take me home?" I paste a smile on my face.

"Sure, no problem."

On the way back, it's Jamie who breaks the silence. "You haven't said much."

I shrug.

"Look, I'll give it to you straight." Jamie steps in front of the chair and squats. "Now we can talk eye to eye." His forehead wrinkles with concern and he stares straight at me.

My teeth chatter and he takes off his leather jacket and drapes it over me. The smell of the leather is intoxicating. What kind of guy brings a leather jacket camping?

"You probably guessed, Kat and I used to be an item."

"I don't have to be a rocket scientist to figure that one out."

He smiles weakly. "Anyways, I got fed up with her flirting with all the guys."

"She's just doing it to make you jealous."

"Well it worked, at first."

"It's still working. You couldn't keep your eyes off her all night."

Jamie blushes. "She's hard to get over."

"And she's a hard act to follow."

"It's like when I gave up cigarettes. I craved one every minute of the day, but I abstained. The cravings became less every day. Eventually, I could look at them, hold them, smell them and I could handle it. I admit she's under my skin, but honest, I'm abstaining."

"Why not just go back to her?" I ask.

"She's no good for me. The second I go back she'll start flirting again. You don't know what that does to a guy, seeing his girl in another guy's arms. I'll get over her because now I've got you."

Adrenalin shoots through me. My heart races as though I've run the marathon. Jamie takes my hand and kisses the palm, sending shivers through me.

"This is a lousy way to start a relationship. I like you, Teresa. I don't know what will happen to us, where we'll go and how far. I just don't want to lose you even as a friend."

Screw my hormones, hello reality. "Jamie, you don't know anything about me. You're on the rebound. Any girl will do." I pull my hand away.

"I don't agree. There's something special about you and I want to find out."

I'm really moved by his words. Now I'm sorry that our night together is ending so soon.

"Are you going back to the party?"

"Na."

"You should go."

"It won't be any fun without you." He pushes me back to my campsite.

My parents are sitting around the fire. I figured they would wait up for me.

Jamie waves goodbye and lets them take over.

"Have a good time?" asks Dad.

"Okay."

"Why are covered in muck?" asks Mom.

"I kind of took a tumble," I mutter.

"Go take a shower before bed," says Mom. "You're not getting mud inside the tent."

"Okay." Mom grabs my stuff for me and as I take a shower, I sing, "I'm gonna wash that man right out of my hair," from the musical *South Pacific.*

When I return to our campsite, Mom asks, "Want me to help you get ready for bed?"

"No, I'm fine." If I want to get my life back, I have to take charge.

Doing anything without help takes double the time and effort. I even surprise myself that I can get into the tent, although I get tangled in the tarp and feel a bit like being caught in a spider's web until I get free. When I make it into bed, exhaustion overtakes me.

Karen rolls over. "Is Jamie a good kisser?"

The Kayak

I throw my pillow at her, but I'm not really mad. It's just none of her business. It's funny, when I'm over tired, I get too wound up to sleep. His words echo in my head. *There's something special about you and I want to find out.* I sigh, deeply. Then it's like I'm pushed under a cold shower. Horseback riding. The gang's going horseback riding tomorrow and I'm left out already. I can just see Kat gloating.

I toss and turn all night. My legs keep cramping. I rub the knots out with my hands. My spine is damaged, but I can still feel my legs, even if they don't work. I don't know what's worse, when nothing happens or bad things happen. Do I really want Jamie that bad? I hardly know him. Do I want to get back at Kat? Absolutely.

5

THE HOT HUMID AIR KEEPS ME tossing and turning all night. When I wake up, Karen is peeling bark off a stick and sulking. "I promise I'll go swimming with you right after I grab some breakfast, okay?"

"Okay, I'll get ready." Karen jumps up and goes into the tent to get changed.

It doesn't take long to finish my bowl of cereal. I'm already in my bathing suit, so I just grab my stuff.

"I'm going to the beach," says Dad. "I'll give you a hand."

"Thanks, Dad," I say. "It's hard work pushing the chair through the sand." Dad wheels me in my wheelchair. My chair has some bells and whistles such as a cup holder, a backpack and a beach umbrella. He pushes me into the shallow water. I slide out and start swimming. Dad takes my wheelchair out of the water and finds a place to set up his umbrella and blanket.

The Kayak

It's not easy floating when my legs are a dead weight, but my arms have gotten pretty strong since I kayak every day. My favourite stroke is the back crawl, but when I try to do it, the waves bury me and I come up choking. Instead, I ride the waves while Karen jumps and dives into them.

There's something magical about the water. All my troubles disappear. It's so invigorating; I can stay in for hours relishing the feeling of weightlessness. It's not until I start to shiver that I decide to get out. Karen loves that I last so long because she's a kid and kids can play forever, oblivious to the cold.

I wave to Dad and he helps me out.

The sun is hot and inviting as we lie down on our towels. I look albino and desperately need a tan, but my mother insists we sit under the umbrella and makes us slather ourselves with sunscreen #50. There's no point in arguing; it's a lost battle. We munch on potato chips, but that just makes me thirsty and I chug-a-lug a litre of water. Dad looks antsy as he drums his fingers on his leg and Mom is fussing and rearranging our stuff.

"Mom, why don't you and Dad go for a walk?"

"And leave you?" She looks hurt, as if I'm trying to get rid of her.

"I'm just going to veg out. Besides, Karen's with me."

"We'll make sandcastles," says Karen.

"Yes, we will," I lie. "Go."

Dad's eyes sparkle. I haven't seen that look in a long time. "Come on Martha." He puts his hand on her thigh.

"Not in front of the children." She swats his hand away, smiling.

I watch them walk along the beach hand in hand. When was the last time I'd seen them stop being parents?

Karen takes off to hang out with some kids she knows further down the beach. I close the umbrella and read. The sun feels good till I suddenly realize I'm again in the shade. "Jamie!" I gulp. I totally didn't expect him to show.

"Hi, Teresa."

"How was riding?"

"Not half the fun if you'd been there."

"I told you, I'm a fish out of water," I say.

"I've got something great to tell you?" He's bursting with excitement.

"What?" I ask.

"While waiting for our horses to be saddled, I wandered inside the arena. They have a class for kids and adults with . . . " he clears his throat, "with special needs."

"I see." I stiffen up.

"It was so cool. These kids were actually riding and I was thinking, maybe you'd want to try. "He senses my uneasiness. "You know, as a challenge."

As a challenge. I used to jump at that, but not anymore.

"I'll think about it," I lie. "Let's go swimming," I say to break the tension.

The Kayak

"You're on."

He picks me up like a sack of potatoes and carries me over his shoulder. I'm punching him with my fists. "Let me down," I cry.

"You want to go down?" mocks Jamie, "then down it is." He dumps me into the water.

I yelp from the cold and splash him in revenge.

"Why you . . . " He splashes me back and soon we are having a splash fight and laugh our heads off until a wave catches us off guard and buries us. We both surface sputtering. I float a little then dive under and pick up a clam shell. He jumps under and holds up a sparkling rock.

"Gold," he cries. "For you."

Fool's gold. I play along. "I'm rich."

I'm cold but I don't want to get out because we're equals in the water.

"I'm turning into a prune," says Jamie.

"Okay," I agree.

We stretch out on the blanket and I close the umbrella. Ah, it feels so good to have the sun on me. The rays energize me. Jamie's on his back beside me. He slides over and his arm and leg are touching mine. If I thought the sun was hot, this is like a blowtorch. I'm embarrassed and overwhelmed at such a strong physical reaction. Is it him or is it because I haven't been touched in such a long time? I figure it's the latter and I pull away and sit up. I better say something. "Want to learn how to kayak?"

"Only if you learn something new too," dares Jamie.

"You're on."

6

I'M UP FOR THE DARE. I figure he means something like sailing.

"I dare you to go horseback riding," says Jamie.

Not this again, I sigh. "Why do you even care?"

"Because it's something I love and the gang always goes. If you learn, you can join us."

"I'll just fall off — then what?"

"You made a deal." Jamie smiles. "Now teach me how to kayak."

I don't want to fight so I just play along. Later, I'll think up an excuse not to horseback ride. "First you have to do the knock-knock test."

"You mean, 'knock, knock who's there?'" he asks.

"Very funny. It's a test to prove that you won't panic if your kayak flips upside down."

"You mean an Eskimo roll?" Jamie asks.

"That's too advanced. For now, this knock-knock test is good enough. When you flip, you stay upside down and extend your hand to the surface and knock on the outside of the kayak three times before releasing your skirt and swimming out and up to the surface."

"That's easy," he says.

"You might be surprised. Once I saw a synchronized swimmer who tried and panicked."

Jamie raises his eyebrows. "No kidding?"

"Let's get started." Jamie helps me into my wheelchair. "My blue kayak's leaning against the birch tree." I point. Jamie portages it into the water. Then he comes back for me. I reach for the basket of kayak attire beside my blanket and hand him a life jacket. "I know you're not used to wearing one of these, but put it on."

He winks. "Fine." He holds out the skirt. "But do I have to wear this?"

"Sorry macho man. The skirt keeps the water out when waves splash in. You don't want to swamp the boat."

"How do I wear it?"

"Step into the skirt, slip it on and tighten up the waist band. When you sit in the kayak, you secure the skirt around the outside of the cockpit."

"But what if I tip? Won't I be trapped?" asks Jamie.

"See that loop at the end?"

"Yeah."

"Well you pull on that and the skirt releases and you are out in a flash."

Jamie does a hula dance in the skirt. He looks so ridiculous, that I burst out laughing. Then he wheels me to the shoreline.

He sets his camera on a tripod and runs back to the kayak. Before I can explain how to get into the kayak, he already has one foot in the boat and the kayak tips. As he sits in the shallow water, I laugh myself silly. *Snap*.

Karen and her friend come to watch the fun. I call out instructions from shore. "Some kayakers hold their paddle behind the seat and distribute their weight evenly to get in. I like to put the paddle in front of the cockpit and with one hand on either side, place my weight in the middle as I get in." Jamie tries again and ends up spitting out water.

"Slowly. If you lean one way with your arm, counterbalance it with your leg." He flips again and again. I can't remember laughing so hard. What I like about him is that he's a good sport about it and keeps on trying. I'm impressed.

Finally, he succeeds and gets in without tipping. "Push off with your hands." I don't even bother giving him a paddle for this exercise. "Make sure you're deep enough to tip." The current takes him out.

"Here goes." He leans to one side and flips the boat. In one second he's up to the surface sputtering.

"Where's the knock-knock?" I ask.

He coughs and treads water. "You're right, gasp. It's not so easy. My instincts make me shoot to the surface." He lets go of the boat and the current pushes it out.

"My kayak," I cry. "Swim after it."

Jamie races after it. He better not lose my kayak. I don't know what I'd do without it. Finally, Jamie catches up to it and holds on.

"Now what?" he calls.

"Kick the kayak into shore and lift one end when you can stand." He does and a torrent of water drains out.

"Sorry about that. I promise it won't happen again," says Jamie.

"Okay," I sigh. "Try again."

He goes through the same routine and once again pops right up to the surface without knocking. "I know, I forgot to knock." He kicks the boat back to shore and empties it. "I'm going to get it right this time." Once again, he gets in and pushes off. "Here goes." He tips.

I'm waiting and waiting for him to come up. I'm getting more nervous by the second. Jamie, where are you? But he doesn't come up and I start to panic. I have to do something. "Karen, help me into the water," I shout. My sister and her friend come running and wheel me into the water. Quickly, I slide out and start swimming as fast as I can to the kayak. Still no sign of Jamie. I reach the boat. "Jamie, where are you?" I call. Just as I get ready to dive under, an arm shoots up and hits the side of the boat, "Knock, knock, knock," and up pops Jamie, gasping for breath and grinning like an idiot.

I splash his face. "You scared me half to death."

He laughs. "I knocked three times didn't I?" he teases.

"It's not humanly possible to hold your breath for so long. How did you do it?" I ask.

"I went under the boat and there was an air pocket. I just waited until I could hear you before coming up."

"Why you . . . " We get into a splashing fight. We are both laughing hard.

"I have a knock-knock joke for you," says Jamie. "Knock, knock . . . "

"Who's there?" I play along.

"Banana," he says. "Knock, knock . . . "

"Who's there?" I say.

"Banana. Knock, knock . . . "

"Who's there?" I say.

"Orange ya glad I didn't say banana?" He smiles.

"Oo," I groan. "That's a kid's joke."

"Teresa, I've done your dare, now you do mine." We're both holding onto the overturned kayak.

"Okay, okay, I'll learn to horseback ride."

Jamie leans over and kisses me. It's a slow long kiss. When we stop and I look ashore, my parents are standing there watching with Karen and one of her friends. Talk about bad timing.

I'm a mixture of emotions — embarrassed, turned-on and overwhelmed. All from just a stupid kiss. I have no privacy. Our first kiss — a free show.

Jamie kicks the kayak to shore, and lifts one end as the water gushes out. I swim back. My parents pretend to be busy, packing up, but I know what they have seen and Karen is blowing kisses at me. I want to swat her.

Jamie puts his camera away and carries the kayak back to the tree, far from shore. Then he breaks the tension by chasing Karen down the beach moving stiffly with outstretched arms like the monster Frankenstein while she squeals with delight and runs away.

This buys me time to figure out how to react.

When Jamie returns out of breath, I pretend that nothing has happened. He is all gentleman and helps me into my wheelchair. I get weirded out and act formal with him. "Thank you for coming down here today. It was very nice of you."

"It was only a kiss. Haven't you been kissed before?" He's not smiling.

"Of course I have, but not in front of my parents," I retort.

Things are awkward between us and we both don't know what to say. Luckily, the gang arrives to play volleyball.

To get his attention, Kat throws Jamie the ball. He joins the game and I'm left on the sidelines watching.

The Kayak

I'm angry as a hornet for being excluded and just itching to sting someone. Kat runs towards me after the out-of-bounds ball. She's distracted when she sees me in her path and is going to trip over a tree limb sticking out in the sand. I should warn her, but I don't.

She goes flying.

7

"Ow," cries Kat sprawled in the sand rubbing her ankle.

Everyone runs over to see if she is okay. She is a drama queen and plays it for all it's worth.

Jamie gets to her first. "Are you okay?" he says, just a little too concerned

"I think I sprained my ankle."

"Does it hurt?" he asks?

"It's throbbing," she says.

"Here let me help you up." When Jamie tries to help her stand she lets out a yell and collapses.

"It hurts too much when I put weight on it. Can you carry me back to my campsite?" She looks at him with big sad eyes.

"Of course." He lifts her in his arms.

At this point I'm feeling very guilty. Then I catch the wicked smile that Kat gives me over Jamie's shoulder as he carries her away. What a faker!

The Kayak

The volleyball game is called and Jamie's friend Pasquali struts over. "Can I, um walk you back to your campsite?"

"I can manage on my own," I say. He looks hurt so I change my mind. "But I would like your company."

He smiles. "Okay if I push?"

It's hard for me to wheel through sand so I put my ego aside. "Sure, Pasquali, that would be nice."

"The guys call me by my last name, but you can call me Mario."

"Okay, Mario."

He pushes in silence. I should try to talk to him since he seems like such a nice guy. "How long are you staying?"

"Not long enough. I've gotta get back to work."

"What do you do?" I ask.

"Construction. I work for my Uncle Luigi. It's the busiest time of year for us."

"Which school do you go to?"

He looks down at his feet. "I dropped out. My Dad hurt his back bad on the job, so my family depends on me. It's okay, I like working with my hands."

We arrive at my campground.

He comes to sit beside me. "Kat told me that you have a huge crush on me."

"What?"

"I need to break this to you gently. Now don't take it bad, but I can't be your boyfriend because . . . " He clears his throat.

"Go on," I say stiffly.

"Because you're not Italian."

"Huh?"

"My Mama would kill me if I went out with a girl who wasn't Italian."

I start to laugh.

"What's so funny?" He looks hurt.

"I thought you were going to say you couldn't date me because I was disabled."

"No way," he says.

"Friends?" I ask.

"Friends," he says shaking my hand.

"Have you known Jamie long?" I ask.

"Jamie, Kat and me grew up together in Ottawa. Our families are all friends and vacation here every summer."

"Long time friends are best," I say. It hits me that I pushed away my friends after my accident. At the time, I couldn't face their pity and I was scared and lost. Now it is too late.

"I gotta go. I promised to babysit my cousins. See ya."

Today I learned a lot about Pasquali. He has a first name and he's a gentleman. I also learned that Kat will stop at nothing to keep me away from Jamie.

The Kayak

I don't hear from Jamie for two long days and I'm so sick of hanging out only with my family. I need to be with people my own age. I make my father drive me around the park, but I don't see the gang either.

I decide to go kayaking to get out of my funk.

It takes me a long time to get into my zone while kayaking. I pass the multi-coloured rocks of black shale, white marble and pink granite. The paddling finally makes me feel alive and I calm down.

The waves and current aren't strong today so I push for speed and distance. I know it's time to turn back because my bladder has a time limit. I do a front sweep with my paddle and out of the corner of my eye, I gasp when I see Jamie sunbathing on the beach. Kat is playing Frisbee so I guess her ankle is okay. Big surprise. She is purposefully near Jamie so that he can't help but watch her every move. And no wonder that he does, as she leaves little to the imagination in her string bikini. Talk about a girl desperate for attention, especially Jamie's. I should feel happy that I finally found him, instead I feel angry that he's not even thinking of me. Out of sight, out of mind.

Suddenly, he waves to me and I feebly wave back.

He shouts so I have to paddle closer to hear.

"How are ya?" he says all cool.

"Okay. I didn't expect to see you here," I say and it's true.

"The gang likes to try different beaches." He brushes his bangs from his eyes.

"Have fun. I have to get back." I start paddling away.

"See you."

"Yeah right," I mutter under my breath.

"How about tomorrow?" he asks.

"I'll have to check my schedule," and I take off full speed, leaving a wake and leaving him guessing. It feels great being back in the driver's seat so to speak.

A motorboat gets too close and nearly swamps me with its wake. I have to quickly turn my boat to ride the wave on a diagonal so that I don't tip. I shake a fist at the driver's back, but he is already too far away to notice. So much for being in the driver's seat.

8

THE SECOND I TOLD MY PARENTS about the therapeutic horseback riding in the area, my mother got on the phone and booked an appointment for me.

"They have an opening at ten this morning," says Mom. "The secretary told me that normally we would have to wait weeks to get in, but a boy got poison ivy and we can have his time slot, sad for the boy of course, but good for us," says Mom all in one breath. "We better hurry."

Mom and Dad are so chipper and enthusiastic about it that I hate to bring them down.

I'd rather be kayaking, but Jamie challenged me to go horseback riding. Challenge used to be my thing. I loved taking chances, doing dangerous and daring sports. It's funny, but I never got hurt doing something like skiing black-diamond runs, doing jumps while snowboarding, or scuba diving in shark-infested waters. Ironically, I got injured doing something in my own neighbourhood.

What would Mr. Rogers have to say about that? Jogging is supposed to be safe and easy, but along came a car and splat. My mother feels super guilty because I had asked her if she would drive me to the mall and she had said that she was too busy so I went running instead. She blames herself, that if only she had said yes, my life would still be normal.

It's weird, but I don't remember anything about the accident. The therapist says that I blocked the traumatic memory because it was too painful to deal with. Whatever. It was a hit-and-run. My parents want the guilty party to be prosecuted and pay for just leaving me lying there on the road to die, but I just want to forget.

"Will you hurry up," says Mom jogging me back to the present. "We need to leave for the stables right away."

"Can I come too?" asks Karen.

"Okay. Tell Dad we're ready," says Mom.

I'm not doing this horseback riding, to get into the Para Olympics, or to win small competitions, or just because Jamie challenged me. I'm doing it for the satisfaction of showing Kat that I can ride too.

A woman in a skirt sits down with me and my parents. "I'm Mary, the co-ordinator. You may be wondering what this riding program is all about. Let me briefly explain. Therapeutic riding has healing or curative powers."

"Yeah, like I'll magically be able to walk again?" I blurt out.

The Kayak

My mother gives me a warning look and my father frowns.

The woman drones on in her professional tone. "You may not be cured by riding, Teresa, but the body receives healthy exercise which brings about improved circulation and muscle tone. Measurable progress is made in restoration of some body functions. It is also great social interaction between peers and it can bring great benefits to the body, mind and spirit."

I tune out as she recites her happy-go-lucky song-and-dance. The office door is open and I can see into the waiting room. Most of the kids look pathetic. Great social benefits abound.

Karen wanders off to get a closer look at the horses.

"What is hippotherapy?" Mom asks.

"Hippotherapy is only done by licensed therapists. It's a passive form of therapeutic riding where the patient sits on the horse and accommodates to the swinging motion." She prattles on.

Am I ever going to ride? I frown. My parents seem totally engrossed by what Mary is saying.

"The function of passive therapy is to have a curative effect on disease and improve psychological and physical conditions."

My parents drink in every word like it's going to change everything.

I stare at a drooling boy slumped in a chair across the hall and interrupt her patter. "How long has that kid . . . " I point at the drooler, "been taking lessons?"

Again, Mary doesn't miss a beat. "We all start at different levels. Since Tony has taken riding with us, he has improved significantly."

Riding would be okay if I could take off into a field and ride like the wind.

Mary continues as I half listen. "The horse must be a well-trained therapy horse. Its stride should be long and even, and it should have a good, comfortable back for riding. The movements of its back should be swinging, not jolting."

I watch the riders through the glass window. *How exciting, walking in circles around a ring and with three helpers. Doesn't get better than that*, is what I am thinking.

Mary hands my mother a clipboard. "But first the paperwork."

Mom fills out the necessary papers and hands it back.

Mary looks it over, then turns to me, "Shall we get you on the saddle, Teresa?"

Before I can say anything, she gets up and takes the handles of my wheelchair and pushes me out the door to the mounting ramp. I nearly gag at the stench of horse manure. It forces me to breathe through my mouth.

"You'll get used to the smell." She gives me a leather belt with loops on it. "Here, put this on. The sidewalkers need the loops to hold onto," says Mary.

I put it on.

"Each individual has to mount by themselves. The method is tailored to their disability. Crawl up the ramp to your horse. Then grab the pommel and cantle and pull yourself prone across the saddle. The instructor and spotter will turn you, so you can push yourself up to a sitting position. It's safe, and makes you somewhat independent."

I'm not exactly thrilled at the prospect.

"Nancy will take over now. Nancy?" she calls. "Come meet Teresa."

"Howdy," says a slight girl in cowboy boots covered in muck.

How hokey — cowboy talk. Does she expect a 'Howdy partner' back?

"Nancy is our top riding instructor and will be in charge of your therapeutic riding."

"I'm ready when you are," says Nancy.

"Teresa needs partial assistance just for today."

"No problem," says Nancy. "We can do an assistive lift from her wheelchair."

"You're in charge." Mary strides off.

A girl with a ponytail as long as the horse's, comes over to help. "Gerta, position the horse in the ramp," orders Nancy.

A third girl comes over to help. "Bonjour, how are you?" she asks with a French accent.

"Bonne," I answer. And I do feel good.

She smiles. "I'm Michelle. I'm very happy you know French."

"Un petite peu."

"That's okay if you only know a little bit," says Michelle.

"Michelle, you spot the off side," instructs Nancy. Cowgirl Nancy stands squarely in front of the horse. I'm worried because she is so tiny and fragile. How is she going to lift me? Nancy lowers the horse's head. My chair is facing towards the head of the horse and the wheels are locked. Gerta places both hands under my shoulder blades, around my back. Her knees dig against me as she lifts me forward from my chair, pivots and lowers me to a side-sitting position on the saddle, while Michelle places her hands around my hips and assists in positioning me.

It's always humiliating for strangers to be handling me. I'll ride just this once, but that's it, I vow.

Gerta adjusts my stirrups. "Your horse's name is Glue."

"Glue?" I echo.

"Yah, he was saved from going to the glue factory and came here instead."

I don't know if Gerta is joking or not, but I keep my mouth clamped shut.

Nancy pulls on the reins and I'm jerked forward. "Don't worry, my job as the leader is controlling the horse. Michelle and Gerta are called sidewalkers." Nancy leads my horse to the arena. She makes a slow wide turn and walks around the arena on the track, keeping away from the other horses.

"The sidewalker's job is just as important as the leader's job, but for different reasons," she explains. "Some riders have very poor balance, may be very nervous, or have little or no muscle power in their legs, where some simply require the emotional support of having someone close by."

But when the horse in front of me suddenly stops, Glue gets too close and bites its rump causing it to rear!

9

As the horse rears and kicks, the leaders and sidewalkers all scramble to separate the two horses and calm them down. Finally, things are getting interesting.

"Way to go," I whisper in Glue's ear. "I'm Teresa. I'm so glad that you were spared from the glue factory," and I pat him. This isn't so bad after all. I see my parents watching through the window. They have such hope in their eyes. Hoping for a miracle.

It suddenly dawns on me that the real purpose of this exercise is so that I can go riding with the gang on a trail, but really, I'm stuck here riding in a barn with three helpers. It's not going to happen. My body sways back and forth to the rhythm of the horse's walk. I have to admit the movement is soothing.

I notice Karen watching. I see the longing in her face. She's dying to ride. My sister always gets the short end of the stick.

I have to convince my parents to let her ride.

The Kayak

The horse ahead lifts its tail and out plops a huge turd. "Oo, gross." I plug my nose with one hand from the stench.

"He's only doing what comes natural, n'est pas?" Michelle smiles.

"Do you want to trot?" asks Nancy.

"Do I." I'm all fired up.

"Ready everybody?" asks Nancy.

"Ready," says Gerta and Michelle together.

"Teresa, tighten up on your reins," says Nancy.

I do. I'm suddenly jerked forward as my horse takes off.

I can feel each step through my chest all the way to my teeth with every bounce on the saddle.

I'm actually exhausted when we slow to a walk.

It's funny, but when I used to dismount a horse BC (Before Chair) I would walk bow-legged. And now, even though my spine is partially damaged and my legs don't work, I still experience tingling and stiffness in my legs. It's been a long time since I felt that way. When I used to run, my legs often felt sore, but it was a good sore, a well-earned sore. I love it. I'm stiff! For once, I feel really alive. However, I am in strong need of a shower, because I definitely smell like horse and sweat.

After we get back I take a shower. Back in the tent, Karen drills me on every detail of my riding class. I patiently answer. She is oozing with jealousy and who can blame her? "How come I can't go riding?"she wonders out loud.

"Because this was a riding class just for invalids," I joke.

"I don't care." Karen ignores — or doesn't get — my sarcasm. "Mom and Dad never let me do anything fun."

"You're right, Karen, it's not fair. Why can't you take riding lessons too? I'll talk to Mom."

"Promise?" asks Karen.

"I promise."

"I owe you one."

Owe me one? What a joke. My sister looks after me day and night, fetching for me, pushing my chair, you name it. And she takes a lot of crap from me. I don't mean to dump on her, but I get so frustrated when I can't do things myself that I often take it out on the closest person to me, mainly my right-hand girl. Poor kid. We can't do a lot of things she would like to do. We can't go to a lot of places because they lack wheelchair facilities. I have to even the score.

"Mom? Can I talk to you?" I ask.

"Sure." She's half-listening as she chops vegetables for a salad.

"Karen wants to take up riding."

"We can't afford both of you," says Mom.

"Then just give Karen lessons," I argue.

"You need it more," she insists.

"Karen needs it too," I say.

"Karen may want it, but she doesn't need it," Mom insists.

Dad joins us and Mom explains the situation.

"The bottom line," says Dad, "is that you need it for your health and health always comes first."

"Take Karen kayaking. She'll like that," says Mom wringing her hands.

"Fine, but I'm going to find a way to get her riding."

I wheel over to Karen who is playing with the dead fire and is itching to find out what happened.

"Well?" she asks.

"I'll tell you in the kayak. Get ready."

Karen carries our paddles down and the rest of the kayak gear is on a bag attached to my wheelchair. We go to where we always leave our kayaks and to our shock they are both gone!

10

DAD AND KAREN DISAPPEAR DOWN THE shore searching for our boats, while I wait with Mom.

I get more anxious with each passing minute. Kayaking is my only outlet. It's also one of the few things I can do with my sister. My parents can't afford to buy one more, let alone two more boats.

Then Karen and Dad return, dragging back our kayaks, holding onto the painters.

"You found them!" I shout.

"Probably some kids took them for a joy ride even though you didn't leave the paddles in the boats." He is annoyed.

"Where were they?" I ask.

"We were lucky. They were washed up on shore, caught in some bushes," says Dad. "If the wind had been going the other way, we would never have seen them again."

"Are they damaged?" I ask.

The Kayak

"That's the beauty of plastic boats. They are hardy," says Dad.

"Thanks, Karen," I say.

"I'm glad we didn't lose them too, you know," she says.

"From now on, we lock up our boats," says Mom. "I have our locks and the chains in the trunk."

"Okay," I say. I'm not going to argue.

"I'll have the locks ready for when you get back. Now you girls go have some fun," says Dad, relieved.

Mom helps me put on my life jacket and skirt. Dad lifts me into my kayak and pushes me off. When Karen paddles over in her purple kayak she asks, "They said no to my riding didn't they?"

"How did you know?"

"Because they are being way too nice."

"Let's just go out and enjoy ourselves, okay?" I paddle backwards until it is deep enough for me to turn around. Then I take off, but have to slow down to wait for Karen. My arms have become so strong from having to wheel myself and pull myself up into my chair. The kayaking has had the same effect. I lead Karen away from our beach and over to the next beach. I don't want Karen to have the feeling that she's constantly being watched by our parents. If we're going to go out and be independent, then we are going to do it right. "Your hands are too wide apart." Karen changes her grip. "That's better."

We pass a man who is fishing. "Catch anything?" I ask.

"Not a bite." He shakes his head.

We continue on. "He's fishing in the wrong place," I say.

"How do you know?" asks Karen.

"Follow the birds. They know where the fish are." We watch as a loon dives then resurfaces with a fish in its beak. "Don't tell the fisherman."

"Why?" asks Karen.

"Once I showed my friend where the fish were and she blabbed to her boyfriend who went straight out with one of those sonar T.V. screens. All he had to do was watch the screen to see where the fish were. Soon he took all the fish in that cove.

"Just like Newfoundland. There were once so many cod that they jumped into your boat. Then they over-fished; now, no more cod."

"Okay, I won't tell. Hey, look at that guy on the wake board. Is he ever cute. Wow, look at him jump over the wake."

"I think he's showing off to you," I tease.

"Really?"

"Absolutely," I say.

"Why do I have to wear this stupid life jacket? It's so bulky and hot," Karen complains.

"Because if you tip . . ."

"I know." Karen rolls her eyes. "Why can't Mom buy me a bikini? She makes me wear an ugly one-piece."

"I'll go shopping with you next time," I promise. "And I'll let you pick out your own bathing suit."

"Thanks," says Karen. "Nothing with flowers. I hate flowers."

"Okay, no flowers." I smile.

The problem with paddling with Karen is she talks non-stop.

"I'm hot. Let's stop and go swimming," says Karen.

I'm hot and hungry too so we stop. Karen can't pull me out so I have to tip near shore and swim out. After Karen lands her kayak, she turns my kayak upside down and lifts the bow while the stern sits on the bottom. The water gushes out. She then joins me. The water is cool and refreshing. We sing songs under water and pop up for air and guess each other's tune. It's a kid's game, but fun.

Karen takes our lunch from its waterproof bag. I grab an egg sandwich and eat it in just a few bites. When I work hard for a meal it always tastes so much better. I have to slither and slide my way back into the kayak while Karen steadies my boat. That's more exhausting than paddling. Not the most graceful way of doing it. Karen pushes me off and shortly follows.

We sing songs as we kayak side by side. It's a good day to take Karen out. The waves are fun to ride, but not so big that we have to work too hard or worry about capsizing. The sun is hot, but there is a nice cool breeze. Everything is perfect.

My eyes feast on the landscape. Nothing is more breathtaking than the rocky northeast cost of Georgian Bay with the weathered granite, the wind-sculpted pines and the whitecaps on grey water. The Group of Seven painted this landscape and captured its beauty forever. At home, I have a poster of Georgian Bay and when I'm feeling low, I picture myself kayaking in its choppy waters.

I've done a little research on my favourite area. "Karen, did you know that the northeast coast stretches for 150 kilometres from Port Severn in the south to the upper corner of the bay at Key Harbour?"

"Nope," she replies.

"This is the Bay of 30,000 Islands and when there is low water, the number could be twice that."

"No kidding?" Karen starts to count islands as we pass. She points at a cottage on an island. "I wish that we could have our own island. How many cottages are there in Georgian Bay?"

"About 10,000. Mostly along the shore and nearby islands that can be reached by boat."

"Aren't you scared that you will get lost?" asks Karen.

"I have a good sense of direction," I say. "But I should always carry a map and a compass. Sometimes, I forget."

The Kayak

We're out for a long time. What do I have to rush back to? Out here, I'm strong and the boss. Karen listens to my every word. I don't want to go back and turn into the child where my parents make all the decisions. But Karen's not as strong as me. She's a beginner kayaker and she's starting to shiver, a sure sign that she's tired and has had enough.

The wind is picking up. Unfortunately, we're going back against it. It's hard work and Karen is whining. Not a fun combination.

"I'm not moving anywhere no matter how hard I paddle."

"Dig deeper with your strokes," I say.

"I'm tired." She stops paddling and the waves sweep her backwards.

"You can't stop paddling," I yell. "You've just lost ground. All that work and you're back to where you were. Keep going."

Karen paddles hard, but she's already exhausted. Now I know that we're in trouble. I should never have taken her out this far. Coming was easy, but going upwind is torture.

Karen starts to cry. "I can't keep going."

Things are getting serious. We have a long way to paddle back and Karen's not moving forward. I could try pulling her, but that would take forever and exhaust me as well. "There's only one solution," I say.

"What?" asks Karen. She looks at me so trustingly. I hate to disappoint her.

"See that island?" I point to the closest island. Sandpipers are running along the beach near the shoreline.

"Yeah?" she shouts over the wind.

"I'm leaving you there."

11

"WHAT?" KAREN'S EYES ARE WIDE.

"You heard me. I'm leaving you here."

Karen is too terrified to speak.

"It's the most sensible thing. You don't have the strength to get back. I'll go with you to the island, make sure you land safely and then I can paddle fast and get Mom and Dad. They'll rent or borrow a motorboat and come and get you."

Karen watches with big eyes, as I leave the island "Don't get lost," she shouts.

"I won't," I yell as I paddle away. Just in case, I look around to engrave the island's position in my head.

I'm not in any danger as I dig in deep and power paddle with all my might. Beads of sweat are on my forehead. My arms ache, but I keep a steady pace. In fact, it feels good to push myself, like I would on a long distance run. Mind over matter. When the mind gives up so does the body. The endorphins released give me a natural high as I ride the waves. I hold my paddle tight as I steer while my kayak breaches like a humpback whale then slaps into the water. I have to concentrate hard so that I don't capsize. I never take the Bay for granted. The waves and currents are to be respected and it takes skill to conquer them.

I can't let up or I'll lose ground, so I dig in deep with my paddle. Slowly, I make progress and I can see our beach. Normally, I would take out my binoculars to see if my parents are waiting on shore, but I don't dare stop paddling for one second with this strong wind. As I get closer, I recognize my mother's big straw hat and my father's fishing hat with all the pins. Wherever, he travels, he collects pins. His hat is tattered and torn, but he won't wear the new one that Mom bought for him. She even suggested that he transfer the pins to the new hat, but he insists that his hat has too many memories to give it up.

My father is pacing and my mother has her arms wrapped around herself. She does this whenever she's worried. They will never trust me to take out Karen in the kayak again and they will never allow her to go out past the buoy on her own. In an attempt to give her freedom, I have taken it away.

"Where's your sister?" screams my mother as soon as I am within calling distance.

"On an island," I shout back.

Dad runs into the water to help me land. "I can do it myself," goes to deaf ears. "Don't worry, Karen's safe," I try to reassure them.

"How could you leave her all alone?" shouts my mother.

I quickly explain while Dad rushes to put me in my wheelchair and pull my kayak out of the water. He ties it up without taking the extra time to lock it. I don't dare say anything. Dad sees a motorboat ready to leave shore and runs down the beach waving like a lunatic. The man stops and Dad frantically explains the emergency. Before I know it, I am carried on board to give directions and we're off to save my sister.

12

No matter how much I try to explain that Karen is in no danger and that she's waiting safely instead of fighting her way back, my parents act like Karen has capsized and is going down for the third time.

I try to make light of the matter. "Hey, the only thing she has to worry about is being eaten by mosquitoes."

Nobody laughs.

I better keep my big mouth shut, I decide.

"You sure we are going the right way?" asks Dad.

"I'm sure. We are going with the wind and I recognize that buoy close to shore," I say.

It's amazing that my long hard paddle back only takes minutes to get to the island by motorboat.

When we get to the island where I left Karen, I immediately see her purple kayak, but Karen is nowhere in sight.

"Where's your sister?" Mom is beside herself.

"She couldn't have gone off the island," I say pointing at her kayak.

Bill, the driver, turns off the motor and raises it while we drift to shore. Dad jumps into the shallows holding the painter and pulls the boat in.

Where is she? I'm left in the motorboat as Dad ties the rope to a spruce tree and everybody else gets out. The search party begins.

"Karen!" shouts my Dad.

Mom runs up and down the shoreline calling Karen's name.

"I'll look for footprints in the sand," calls Bill.

Out walks Karen from the woods. Mom runs to her and gives her a bear hug, nearly squeezing her to death. She might have been better off meeting a real bear. My father and Bill hurry over.

"What were you doing in the woods?" asks Dad.

Karen blushes. "Nothing."

They walk back in the water towards the motorboat. "She was bushing it, Dad," I say, knowing exactly why she would blush and say, "nothing."

"Oh," answers Dad. He turns to Karen. "Well, I'm glad you're safe."

"Ladies, into the motorboat," calls Bill. Dad helps him tie Karen's kayak to a ski line attached to the motorboat. That takes a few minutes and soon the motor roars into action and we take off towing the kayak behind us.

Dad offers to pay Bill for his troubles but he refuses.

"Tell you what," says Bill. "Tomorrow morning, I'll take your family out in my fishing boat with my wife and daughter. My daughter's around the same age as Teresa. I'm sure that they will hit it off. You can bring the soft drinks."

"That's a deal," says Dad, and they bore us to death talking about fishing the rest of the way back.

Later that evening, Karen retells the story that by now is quite an adventure. She has a vivid imagination. She talks about me capsizing even though I did it on purpose to get out of the boat to have our swim. She brags about fighting the wind and gigantic waves. You would have thought that she had just paddled in a typhoon. But I grin and bear it because it is my fault after all and there is nothing I can do about it. The only good thing that comes out of this is Bill's promise to take us all fishing tomorrow. Even though this is not my idea of fun, I can watch carefully and see new and interesting places that I can kayak to later on my own. I wonder what Bill's daughter is like? It will be fun hanging out with someone my own age for the day.

In the distance, I hear a coyote howling. Others join in. Each has its own voice and I'm fortunate to hear them. I look out the window at the full moon. The stars are shining bright. It's truly magnificent. The beauty of it all makes me feel happy to be a part of it. For once I'm grateful. At first, all night sounds kept me awake, but now they are music to my ears and they lull me to sleep. I dream of running through the forest. It's such a vivid dream. My legs are muscular and strong and I'm moving so fast that it is exhilarating.

When I begin to wake up, I forget that the dream isn't possible and I try to stand. But when my legs don't respond, I awake fully and the joy is jolted from me. Reality sinks in. I close my eyes and try to recapture the dream, but it has already faded.

"Everybody up," calls Dad. "The early bird catches the worm." I can hear Karen complaining. Hungry and grumpy, I get ready.

Bill meets us at the waterfront and leads us to his fishing boat, tied up at the wharf. It is a big pontoon boat.

We get on board and there is enough room for me to manoeuvre my wheelchair. Bill introduces us to his family. His wife, Mitzy is a rinse blonde. She seems an expert on shopping as she tells us the price of everything. But the surprise is the daughter.

"Hello, Kat," I say.

"Hello, Teresa," she says smiling, but I can see that her eyes are not.

13

It feels like I am in a lion's den. How do I stay alive? I must show my superiority to the lion. Look her straight in the eye, stand my ground and show her who is boss. A lion tamer makes a lot of noise, shouting and flicking his whip. He can't show any weakness. The tamer claims his territory. I'm not about to scream, shout and whistle, but I'm not going to quiver and whisper either. I look the enemy straight in the eye, wheel right up to her and speak with confidence. "Oh, good, just us two — no guys. We'll have a girls' day out."

For a moment, Kat looks like the wind had been taken out of her sails, but she recovers quickly. "Boys can be such babies and such a pain at times."

"Amen," I say. Maybe we can be friends after all, I wonder.

But it doesn't take her long to get to what's really on her mind.

"What do you think of Jamie?" she asks.

Does she expect me to get jealous? I just started going out with him. "He's okay," I say. "I've had better," I exaggerate.

"You know, he is only being nice because he feels sorry . . . "

Before she actually gets to finish her unbelievable comment, my mother comes over with two fishing rods. "Sorry to interrupt, but Bill wants to know if either of you want to fish?"

"Count me out," says Kat.

Sometimes a parents' blindness can be a good thing. "I'll take the red one!" I say too cheerfully.

"Really?" she asks.

"I'll catch and throw it back. I'm up to trying something new," I say. Any excuse to get away from this piranha who kills by taking little bites out of me. But piranhas aren't that effective without their school attacking with them. I wheel myself over to the men who are already fishing.

"Need any help, little lady, baiting your hook?" asks Bill.

"No, I'm fine." I squirm as I put the wiggly worm on the hook. I'm not going to act weak. The weak get eaten alive. I put my line into the water.

Karen has finished exploring the boat and my father baits her hook. Every few minutes she peeks to see if she has caught a fish and reels her line in.

Dad is just in it for the fishing and the jock talk. "How about them Leafs?" asks Dad.

"We should trade every last one of them," says Bill.

It's not even hockey season. I roll my eyes.

Mitzy is busy mixing drinks for the adults. I see that she's drinking them faster than she's filling them. She's laughing too loud and spills her drink all over my father's pants.

"Oopsy," she laughs. She goes to blot the stain out of my father's pants, but my father puts up a hand that in no uncertain terms says, stop.

My father's face turns red. "It's okay, I can do it myself."

Mom is watching like a hawk.

"No harm done," says Dad when Bill looks angrily at his wife. They go back to fishing, and Mom goes back to reading or at least pretending to read. But I see that Mom keeps checking on Mitzy's whereabouts.

I've nicknamed her 'Ditzy Mitzy'. She pours herself another one and toasts herself.

I'm starting to understand what makes Kat tick. Having a mother like that can't be easy. It doesn't mean that I like her any better than before, I just feel sorry for her.

Bill shows Karen how to cast. "Reel 'er in nice and easy," he explains. "I never could get Kat interested in fishing," he says. He looks so happy teaching Karen.

Meanwhile, Kat has fallen asleep while tanning on the deck and she's quickly turning red as a lobster. Should I wake her? I decide to let her roast.

We pass the most beautiful beach, tucked away in a small bay. The sand is pure white and the beach is deserted. All my senses come alive. I just have to come back here on my own. Now I pay attention to where we are. "Do you have a map?" I ask.

"Sure, little lady." Bill gets up and gives it to me.

"Where we are?" I ask.

He studies the map and puts his thumb on the spot. "Right here."

I make a mental map in my head. This trip is worthwhile after all. I just discovered my own Eden. I will be back.

Lunchtime is tense because I have to make chit-chat with Kat to appease the parents.

"What sports do you like?" I ask.

"Basketball," says Kat. "I'm on the A-team at our school," she brags. "I won MVP last season. I just love playing."

"I'm on a basketball team too," I say.

Kat looks at me surprised.

"Wheelchair basketball. My team is up for the Provincials." I don't have to mention that I don't like basketball and that I am a sub and I hardly go anymore.

"Oh . . ."

One point for the good guys. We all turn and stare at Mitzy as she bumps into the food tray and collapses onto the deck.

14

Bill is the first one to reach Mitzy. He lifts her from the deck and places her onto a bench.

"Is she okay?" asks my mother.

"Just a bit too much sun," says Kat covering up for her mother.

"And it looks like you're getting too much sun as well," says my mother.

Kat takes a look at her sunburned arms and legs and swears under her breath as she reaches for her bathrobe.

Moments later, she applies a cool cloth to her mother's forehead and soon enough, Mitzy is back to normal.

As we come close to shore, we can see Jamie waiting — obviously for Kat, not me. Our families say their good-byes and Kat makes sure that she has the last word.

"Did I tell you that Jamie and I are going for a hike?"

Jamie, now close enough to hear, looks embarrassed.

Kat hurries over to him giving him a quick kiss. "I'm ready for that hike."

I watch them walk off. Kat looks triumphant and Jamie looks like he can't get away fast enough.

15

A WHILE LATER, KAREN IS STRETCHED OUT on a blanket with a new friend. They are painting their nails. She has no trouble making friends like I do. When I wheel over, Karen introduces me. "Teresa, this is Margriet."

She has big brown eyes, and wears her hair in a thick long braid down the middle of her back.

"Hi, Margriet. Is that a Dutch name?" I ask.

"Ya, but I was born here. My parents came from the Netherlands."

"Cool," I say.

The girls go back to painting their nails.

On the beach, Jamie is taking pictures of the guys in the gang playing soccer. He's ignoring the girls spread out on their towels to sunbathe. He sees me and heads towards me.

"Karen, give me some privacy, please?" I beg.

"Fine." Karen takes off with Margriet.

"Hi, Jamie. How was your hike?"

"I had a fight with Kat. Listen, I want to apologise. I had no idea that you were on Kat's boat. I know what you must be thinking."

"You don't owe me anything."

"I feel like a jerk." He shuffles his feet. "Let me make it up to you. Want to go out tomorrow afternoon so I can explain?"

While Jamie is making his apology, Kat is approaching. "Hi, Kat," I say.

Jamie glares at her.

"I came over to say that I was sorry about the hike. We shouldn't have gone if Teresa couldn't join us," says Kat.

Jamie's smile embraces her. "I knew that you would see what was right."

Is she being manipulative, or is Jamie being gullible?

"I was about to tell Jamie that I'm riding tomorrow morning at nine," I say.

"Really?" asks Jamie. His eyes light up. "Can I come and watch?"

"Sure."

"How do you do the riding?" he asks. "I mean, without falling off."

"There are three helpers, a leader and two sidewalkers to spot me."

"See you tomorrow at the stables," he says to me and walks away with Kat.

But then Kat turns around and smiles at me and I just know she's up to something.

16

I WAKE UP IN THE MORNING WITH a book on my chest and the flashlight batteries dead. I wheel to the washroom and wash up. I have bags under my eyes. It's impossible to sleep in while camping in a tent. The light pours in at six and Dad is snoring. Mom grunts through her morning stretches and Karen sleeps on the diagonal. No matter where she starts out, she ends up kicking me either in the head or side.

I read, but find that I'm reading the same page over and over. All I can think about is Jamie coming to watch me ride. I wish that he would have waited until I had a few more lessons.

Mom finishes her exercises then begins to get breakfast ready. Meanwhile, Dad heads for the washroom. Then Karen wakes up, throws on some clothes and takes off on her bike.

Even though Mom makes my favourite breakfast —
French toast — I can't eat it. I'm too revved up about
riding.

My parents drop me off at the stable and I insist that
they go off by themselves. No way do I want them hanging
around if Jamie is coming to watch. I say goodbye to
them.

I wheel over to the ramp, get on, and snake up to a
polka-dot horse that Cowgirl Nancy, my leader from last
time, has led over. It is spotted white on black.

"Howdy Teresa, you've got Dalmatian today."

"Hi, Dalmatian." It does look like the dog — in
reverse — they are black on white. "What happened to
Glue?" I ask.

"Glue has the day off. Horses need rest just the way
people do."

"Fair enough. I just want to make sure that he is okay,"
I say.

Nancy holds the reins. "Grab the stirrups and pull
yourself up to a prone position, then reach across the
saddle and pull yourself across on your stomach."

Nancy and Michelle turn me, so I can push myself
up to a sitting position. It's not easy and I'm sweating
buckets.

"I'll help you sit up," says Nancy.

Next she takes the reins and leads me into the arena.
I'm happy to see Michelle from last time as she stands

at my side. "Bonjour. This time you are a pro, non?" she teases.

I like her. "Oui, but I still want you by my side," I say.

"We'll get going in a minute," says Nancy. "We're just waiting for our volunteer to be our other sidewalker."

"Where's Gerta?" I ask.

"Gerta? She's busy feeding the horses. Don't worry. The new volunteer will spot you."

As she says this, Kat approaches. *You have got to be kidding,* I say to myself. But to Kat, I say "Kat! What are you doing here?"

17

"I THOUGHT IT WOULD BE NICE TO volunteer," Kat says.

Nancy interrupts. "Ready, sidewalkers? Let's get started." We start walking around in a circle. Kat is watching the visitor's window more than she is watching me.

I look at the window and Jamie waves at me. I wave back. He also waves at Kat. She blows him a kiss.

This annoys me, so I click my tongue, and in a flash, Dalmatian is running — and so is Kat — trying to keep up.

Nancy pulls hard on the reins, yelling, "Whoa!" Soon, she has the horse in control. "What on earth do you think you're doing? You could have fallen off," she says sternly.

But I don't care because Kat is red in the face, her clothes are covered in mud and she's bent over trying to catch her breath.

"Trotting never felt so fast when I was riding, but when you are running, whew! That feels really fast," says Kat.

"You'll get used to it," says Nancy.

"I don't get it," says Kat. "I play basketball and am in pretty good shape."

"It takes practice and technique. Breathe from the belly not the chest and absorb more in the knees," says Nancy.

"I'm sorry," I say in what I hope is my most apologetic voice.

We do a few laps in the arena and I bide my time. "I used to ride and I love to run. Is it okay if I try trotting?" I ask, innocently.

"Are you up to it, Kat?" asks Nancy.

I can see that Kat doesn't want to lose face. "Yeah, sure," she says.

"For a short distance," says Nancy. "But I always warn my sidewalkers first and tighten up on my reins to lead the horse. You also need to tighten up on your reins."

"Thank you," I say.

"Get ready to trot sidewalkers," says Nancy as she adjusts her grip on the reins.

"Ready," they both say.

Nancy starts to run and Dalmatian takes off. I'm loving the speed and the fact that Kat keeps slipping on the sawdust. She's also panting. All too soon we're back to a walk.

"Hey, ha, you are good in the saddle," compliments Nancy. "You know, it's such a nice day, why don't we leave the barn and go for a trail ride?"

I can't believe my ears. "You bet," I say, enthusiastically.

The feeling of the sun on my face and the wind blowing through my hair while riding through the woods is calming. The interesting thing is that there is plenty of room for me and Dalmatian with our leader along the narrow dirt path, but not for poor Michelle and Kat as sidewalkers. They are off the path. Michelle is okay because she's wearing jeans, but Kat is in shorts and walking in thorny raspberry bushes and scratchy thistles. Kat is sweating, swearing under her breath, and looking quite miserable.

"Can we trot again?" I ask.

"Sure," says Nancy. "Ready to trot, sidewalkers?"

"Ready," they both answer, except Kat doesn't look too thrilled. I tighten my reins and brace myself for the jerky movement to come.

We begin to trot. Nancy and Michelle are sprinting easily and are at ease spotting me at a faster pace, but Kat looks scared that the horse might step on her. She is desperately trying to keep up. By the time we return to the stable, I'm glowing and Kat is a dishevelled mess.

Jamie is waiting for me, taking pictures. I dismount and join Jamie in the waiting room. Kat moves on to her next rider.

"Man, you were amazing," he says.

"Thank you."

"Wanna go for ice cream?" he asks.

"Sure, I'll meet you back here in a few minutes. There is something that I have to do first. Wait here!"

Moments later, I find Cowgirl Nancy.

"Howdy, Teresa. Did you enjoy your ride?

"I sure did. But I came to ask you a question?"

"Spit it out."

"Nancy, could my sister Karen help with the horses while I'm taking riding lessons?"

"Sure, we need all the volunteers that we can get. She can clean the stables, feed the horses and help groom them."

"If she volunteers, can she also ride for free?" I ask.

"Before and after classes only," she says.

"You're the best." I squeeze her hand.

Karen is nearby busy watching the horses.

"Karen?"

She jumps. "Oh, I didn't see you. "

"Great news. My instructor gave you permission to ride before and after classes," I say.

"Really?" Karen's face is flushed with excitement.

"But you have to look after the horses."

Karen hugs me. "I'm going to ask if l can start right away." She is off in a flash.

"Bye, I'll see you later," I call to her.

Then I turn to Jamie. "I'm ready when you are." And I give him a big smile.

18

"Hurry up, we're packing," says Mom.

"What? asks Karen.

"Are we going home?" I feel alarmed. The thought of not kayaking everyday and sitting in my bedroom makes me shudder.

"No, this is great news," says Mom as she takes down the clothesline. "I can't believe our luck. That huge campsite right off the beach is empty. Apparently, a family booked it for a month, stayed one night and left. They must be crazy. It means we don't have that long walk from our campsite down the hill to the waterfront. It will be so much easier."

Dad is busy taking down the tarp. "Karen, give me a hand."

"Are we close to the washroom?" asks Karen.

"Yes, fortunately," answers Dad. "Teresa can easily wheel herself there."

I go into the tent and pack up my things. It's amazing how fast we break camp. It takes so much longer to set up. Soon we are in the car and drive to our new camping spot.

"It's gorgeous," sighs Mom.

"So convenient," says Dad.

"I love it," declares Karen.

I have to admit, that I love it too. We're level to and right across from the main beach. Our campsite faces Georgian Bay and the rocks. The view is breathtaking. Most important, I can come and go on my own as I please. I'm so happy.

The air is still and humid. Sweat pours down me as I help hand things to Mom.

Dad strings a tarp between two trees over our picnic table. I can't wait to jump into the water. Our site is all white sand.

"Hurry up," I complain. "I'm hot."

"That's the beauty of this site," says Dad. "You can go by yourself to the beach. Call me on your walkie-talkie if you have any trouble."

"Okay, Dad," I say, excited. The tent is up and I set up my sleeping bag and put on my bathing suit.

I wheel myself to the beach.

The air is still and stifling. Karen joins me. "Whew, I slipped away. Mom would have me helping her all day if she had her way."

The Kayak

"Don't I know it," I say. "Want to go for a dip?"

"You bet." I can get in and out of my wheelchair by myself, positioned in the shallow water. But I need Karen to safely put it on shore, away from the waves.

The cool water is so refreshing. I play in the waves laughing with Karen. She is happy to jump in and out of them forever. I take off and swim long and hard without a care in the world. The dark blue water against the sky makes me wish I were a painter and could capture this beauty on canvass forever.

The day goes by quickly. I love the fact that I can go back to my campsite whenever I want and not just take things down to the beach for the day.

After a perfect day, I relax at our campsite. Watching the sunset from our picnic table is breathtaking.

"Mom, I'm cold. Will you get me a sweater?" I ask.

"Sure, honey. Boy it's getting gusty," says Mom.

The wind picks up and our dishes blow off the table. Karen chases after them. The tarp comes loose and starts to flap. Dad jumps into action and fixes the tarp. Sand is blowing everywhere, in my eyes, my mouth, and my hair.

"It feels like we're in the desert during a sandstorm," I say.

"What?" shouts my mother over the wailing wind.

"A sandstorm," I shout.

Our clothesline blows down and our stuff is blowing everywhere. Mom, Dad and Karen are running all over the place. Nobody would believe this if I tried to tell them what happened. I have to capture this on video. I get the camera and video everything. I wish Jamie was here to do it.

Mom is madly running after our clothes. Karen runs blindly into the tent and it collapses. Dad runs back to help her.

"Karen, hold the tent while I double peg it," yells Dad over the wind.

Dinner is ruined. All the food on the picnic table is covered in sand, blown to the ground or disappeared out of sight.

Mom talks to one of the neighbours. She comes back mad as a hornet. "The neighbours all know something that we don't know."

"What?" I ask.

"The reason that this spot was empty because anyone who knows about this site doesn't want it."

"Why?" I ask. "Is it haunted?"

"Don't be ridiculous. Apparently, it's the windiest, most open and vulnerable spot in this campground. That's why the last family left."

I can hardly see because of the sand blowing in my face.

A grey-haired man comes over carrying something. "It's only this bad when the wind is blowing northwest and there is a gale. Last night and tonight are those times.

I offered to help the last family that stayed in your site, but they couldn't get out of here fast enough," he chuckles. "You'll be fine once you funnel the wind away from you."

"Thanks," says Dad.

Soon other neighbours bring over extra tarps and show us how to set them up properly. They tie them to trees in front of the picnic table and tent, so that they slope upward and funnel the wind and sand over the table and tent. With the extra tarps up, the site is far from comfortable, but is tolerable. We thank our neighbours and say, good night.

Exhausted, we retreat into the tent. No way can I sit outside with that strong wind. The evening drags as we sit inside the tent playing cards. Later, I wheel myself around the campground looking at other sites. Some people are still up. Yes, it's windy, but they can still sit around their campsites without being buried alive in sand. When I get back to our tent, I ask Mom, "Who told you that this site was available?"

"Bill told us that his daughter Kat said to make sure that we hurried over to get this campsite before anyone else grabbed it up because it was the perfect site. I guess that she didn't know about it being the windiest spot in the entire campground."

Oh, Kat knew all right, I stew.

"We can't stay here. I'll ask your father to go back to the park office and see if we can move back to our old campsite."

Dad drives to the park office. When he returns he is not looking very happy.

"What happened?" asks Mom.

"Our old campsite is already taken and there is nothing left that is wheelchair accessible."

"What do we do now?" asks Mom.

"It's late. First thing tomorrow, we will have to go home," says Dad.

I sit awake in my sleeping bag. *You got me Kat. You got me good and I owe you one.*

19

THE NEXT MORNING, THE LAKE IS calm and there is zero wind. Once again our site is paradise. It's as if last night's gale had never swept through our campsite.

My family sits around the picnic table looking tired and miserable.

"We're not leaving," I say, defiantly.

"But last evening was chaos," says Mom.

"The wind doesn't come from that direction very often. When it's calm, this site is perfect."

"What if the wind changes?" asks Mom.

"Now we know what to do," I say. "We'll keep the tent double-pegged and we'll leave up all of the extra tarps," I say.

"It is a sight for sore eyes," says Mom. "But I'm with Teresa, I want to stay."

Dad shakes his head no. "I still say that we should cut our vacation short."

"Dad, I thought you taught us not to be quitters."

My father looks sheepish. "You do have a point."

"And I took a video last night."

"No," cries Mom.

"Let me see," says Karen.

I turn on the video camera and soon we are howling as we watch Mom chasing clothes, and Karen running blindly into the tent, collapsing the tent, and Dad running from tarp to tarp.

"It's hilarious," says Mom.

"We should enter it in the show for the funniest video," says Karen.

Dad is wiping his eyes from laughing so hard.

"Please can we stay?" asks Karen. "I want to go to the stables with Teresa today."

"Okay," says Dad. "Teresa convinced me. We're staying."

We finish breakfast and I promise to tidy up so that the others can take their showers.

I'm just drying the last dish when Kat walks down the pathway heading in my direction. There goes my tranquil morning.

"How's your campsite?" she asks innocently.

"It's gorgeous. I can't thank you enough. And so convenient. I don't have to stay on the beach all day because I can go back and forth on my own," I babble.

Somehow the answer isn't what she expects. "You didn't find it windy?" Kat looks confused.

"No because we funnelled the wind away from us by the use of tarps. We were perfectly fine."

"Oh," says Kat controlling her disappointment.

"I have to run." I say and watch as Kat is again taken off balance.

"What's the hurry?"she asks.

"I have to get ready for riding this morning. Catch you later."

Kat stands there stunned as I wheel into the tent, or at least try to. With all of the extra tarps and pegs, I become a tangled-up puppet. So much for a graceful exit.

My parents drive Karen and me to the stables. Karen is so excited. Today she is one of my sidewalkers, as one of the volunteers called in sick. I'm not thrilled about walking in a circle, but then I start to stroke my horse and sway with its rhythm, and soon I begin to listen to the lesson and enjoy the ride. Karen chatters away like a chipmunk. It's nice to see her so happy.

After my lesson, Karen removes the saddle and brushes the horse's flank in small circles. She is totally engrossed.

"Can I help?" I ask.

"Sure. Grab a brush."

I take a brush off the hook in the stall and brush where I can reach — the legs mostly.

Nancy calls, "Karen, shovel out Lone Ranger's stall, okay?"

"Okay," says Karen. Crossing to the other stall, she smiles as she shovels out the dung and straw. Funny, how she enjoys doing this, but ask her to clean the toilet at home and she has a fit.

I talk to my horse while I groom. "Good boy, Dalmatian." He neighs when I brush him. I find the rhythmic movement of my stroking his flanks hypnotic and soothing.

When I'm done, my parents take me back to our tent. Karen stays at the stable to go riding now that the lessons are done.

"I need to go to town and buy more tarps so that I can give our neighbours back their tarps," says Dad.

Mom yells after him, "And buy some more bread. I need to make sandwiches."

"Okay, dear." Dad drives off.

"Mom really? After last night in the sandstorm, you want to make 'sand wiches'?" It's really not all that funny, but after the night we just had, Mom and I burst out laughing.

20

"Can I go kayaking?" I ask.

"Sure," says Mom.

"I'll help you get ready." Dad heads off to get my kayak where it is chained to a birch tree.

I'm determined to explore. I head away from our campground, past the park boundaries and past many cottages and islands. I'm feeling great as I paddle hard fighting the wind. I love the feeling of pushing myself.

About two kilometres from the campground, I decide to explore some islands and weave between them. They are beautiful with their rugged rocky shores. The sun reflects off the white granite. Evergreens blow in the wind. Close to shore, small fish, probably sticklebacks, dart amongst the weeds. I'm hot and I splash the cold refreshing water over my face. Droplets trickle down my neck and I stop to drink from my water bottle. I've never been in this area before.

Because I'm tiring, I head back. But as I paddle, nothing looks familiar. I should have kept taking my bearings before I explored all of these little islands. I turn around and head the other way, but still, don't know where I am. I'm getting hungry, tired and cold. Now I'm feeling anxious. I pass the island with the seagulls again. I've been going in circles. The seagulls cry and circle above me. One swoops straight at my head, screeching. "What the . . . " I duck. It comes at me again. "I don't believe it." I hold my paddle above my head so that it doesn't claw me, and it attacks my paddle instead. While it's circling for another attack, I paddle away as fast as possible. It follows me for half a kilometre and keeps screeching and swooping down at me. It must be nesting.

Finally, it circles and heads off. I sigh and look around. I'm all alone. No other boats are in the vicinity. I'm exhausted and I don't recognize the area at all. I'm not turning back to get attacked again by a deranged seagull, so I decide to land as I know I have to rest. The truth is, I'm lost.

I can't find a sandy beach to land on so I'll have to take my chances landing at a stony shore. In the shallows, the waves beat my kayak sideways against the rocks. I tip and pull the loop of my skirt to get out. I land on a sharp stone that jabs into my back. I grit my teeth. I scrape my knees trying to get my kayak higher onto the island shore.

The Kayak

I manage to retrieve my paddle and pull my upside-down kayak partially up onto the granite, but each time a wave comes in, the boat smashes against me. I have to get it higher up. I'm exhausted, but I can't ruin my kayak.

Inch by inch I pull the kayak up until finally the waves can't reach it. I tie it to a tree and pull out my dry sack to try my walkie-talkie. I know that I am out of range, but I try anyway. I collapse on the rocks, my legs bleeding. I'm breathing heavily. My kayak is full of water trapped beneath the seat and the buoyancy bladders. There's no way I can get the water out. I'm stuck here on the island.

I start to cry and I can't stop sobbing. I never really cried after the accident. I held in all of the pain. Finally, I let everything pour out of me, my sorrow, my frustrations, and my loss. After a long time, my tears are dry.

A turkey vulture circles above me, decides I'm not dead and flies away. I'm bruised, hungry and scared, but purged. And very much alone.

21

THE SUN IS ANGLED BEHIND THE trees putting me in the shade. I start to shiver.

A motorboat goes by. I yell at the top of my lungs, but the wind swallows my cries. I have to get the driver's attention. I wave like crazy, but the boater thinks I'm just waving a friendly hello. He waves back and to my disappointment, keeps going.

I watch as the sun goes down. It's getting late. Mom and Dad must be worried by now. I stare out at the water and shiver.

Another boat goes by. *Look at me. Why won't you look at me?* I don't have a flare or matches, I can't jump up and down, and they can't hear me above their motor and the howling wind. What should I do? I watch helplessly as the boat becomes a dot on the horizon. If only my kayak wasn't full of water and upside down, maybe I could find my way back.

The Kayak

The later it is, the chances of boats coming by are slimmer. What will I do when it gets dark? I'll need to build a fire, but I can't collect wood and I don't even have any matches.

I bury my head in my hands.

Then I hear another boat in the distance. It may be my last hope. I can't let this one get away. I'm not going to spend a night alone here.

As the motorboat passes near my island, I wave my arms in big sweeps. The driver waves back. It's a guy. He's going to keep on going just like the other driver.

Drastic times call for drastic measures.

I take off my bikini top and wave it as high as I can.

22

Sure enough, he stops.

I quickly put my top back on. He looks about twenty, tanned, broad shoulders, wearing a huge grin. Now I'm embarrassed.

"My legs . . . I'm shipwrecked."

He looks at my legs and his smile disappears. He looks very serious. "They sure got banged up."

He doesn't know that I can't walk permanently. He thinks that I just hurt them. I look down at my bruised, scraped and bloodied legs. No wonder he thinks that. I don't bother correcting him.

"Shipwrecked?" He shakes his head. "You've been reading too many novels. Why did you put your top back on?" he teases.

I blush. "I needed you to stop," I sputter.

"And it worked." He smiles, showing beautiful white teeth and an adorable dimple.

"Will you help me?" I ask.

Without saying another word, he scoops me up carefully, like I'm made of glass, and places me into his motorized rowboat.

He hands me my paddle, skirt, life jacket and dry sack and then unties my kayak, picks up one end with ease and drains the water. Then he flips it over and ties it to the boat.

"I'm so lucky that you were boating this way," I say.

He pulls on the motor throttle and the motor purrs. It's music to my ears. He puts a blanket across me and tows my boat. He's a man of few words. "Where to?"

"Killbear Provincial Park."

He whistles.

"What?" I ask.

"You're a long way from there."

"Really?" Staring at the landscape, I don't recognize where I am. "I'm Teresa."

"Hi, I'm Jozef, but my friends call me Zef."

"Hi, Zef."

After a time, in this silent man's company, I begin to recognize landmarks. "We're going the right way," I say.

"Did you doubt me?"

"It did cross my mind." My parents for sure will be looking out for me. They'll have a fit if they see me being towed. "There's Cousin Island." I point, "We're getting close to my beach. Will you do me a big favour?" I ask.

"What?" he asks.

"Will you lift me into my kayak?"

"Why?"

"So that my parents won't know that I needed rescuing."

He nods and turns off the motor. He pulls in my boat and gently lowers me into the cockpit. I secure my skirt around the outer rim and he hands me my paddle.

"You okay?" he asks.

"Better than okay." I try not to stare at him. I can't help but notice his muscles and flat stomach. This is a guy who works out.

He watches from a distance until I safely reach shore, then he takes off. I'm glad that my wheelchair is sitting in the shade out of sight.

When I land, Mom starts shouting at me. "We were just about to get a boat to look for you. You had us worried, you know."

"Sorry. I just lost track of time." I feel bad about lying. Mom gets my wheelchair and Dad helps me out of the kayak and into my wheelchair.

Mom gasps. "What happened to your legs?"

"I had to make a pit stop and when I pulled myself up on the rocks . . . I let her make her own picture. The less said the better.

"Are you okay?" Mom frets.

"I think so. Hey, it's part of doing sports, you get a few scrapes and bruises — right, Dad?"

"Right." Dad is proud of his soccer scars, triumphs of his youth. "Next time get out at a beach with sand, not one with rocks."

"If there had been one around, I would have, Dad."

"Better still, don't go out so long so that you need to make a pit stop."

"Okay, Dad." There's no point in arguing.

Dad has a long list of do's and don'ts, but my mind drifts because I just met the most incredible guy. Then it hits me, I never gave him my full name or my campsite number. Killbear is a big place. Will he remember which beach I landed at? Will I ever see him again?

23

THE NEXT DAY, THE GANG IS back playing volleyball.

I'm happy to be distracted when Karen brings over her friend.

"Hi, Margriet. Nice to see you again."

"Help us with our quiz from our magazine?" she asks.

"Sure." I shrug.

"Who would you choose? Mr. Dependable, but boring or Mr. Drop Dead Gorgeous, the player?" reads Margriet.

"I would definitely go for the player," says Karen.

"Me too," says Margriet. "Who would you choose Teresa?"

Who would I choose? Before I can speak, a shadow is cast over me and I look up shielding the sun from my eyes with my hand.

Margriet stands up and hugs the man. "Teresa meet my brother, Zef."

"Oh!" My heart is beating fast. I should have guessed. Zef and Margriet have the same dimple and white teeth when they smile. Relief floods over me. I thought I'd never see him again. Our eyes lock.

"Do you two know each other?" asks his sister.

"I bumped into him while I was kayaking," I say grinning like *Alice In Wonderland's* Cheshire cat.

"I liked what you had on?" he teases.

Heat rises to my cheeks.

"What's going on here?" asks Karen suspiciously.

"Nothing," I say, but I can't help smiling.

He extends his hand. His grip has strength and his hand is warm.

My wheelchair is out of sight behind a tree in the shade so that the metal doesn't get too hot. I'm sitting on a blanket. He doesn't know that I'm handicapped. But why should I care? I don't even know him.

Before long, Zef joins us on the blanket. "What's this?" He picks up the magazine. "Ten ways to drive your man wild?" He has a twinkle in his eye as he stares intensely at me.

Margriet grabs the magazine away from him. Zef digs into his pocket and pulls out some change. "Why don't you girls go for some ice cream?" He doesn't have to ask twice.

His hand brushes my arm and it's on fire. "Are you cold?" he asks.

I look at him and he seems unaffected by our closeness. "No, I'm fine."

"Here, take my shirt." He slips his shirt off over his head and I can't help but stare at his muscles. He holds his white tee shirt out to me. "Put it on."

I slip it over my bathing suit. I like the way that it smells of him. He wears a pine-scented aftershave.

"Do you like camping?" he asks.

I become tongue-tied. I wish that he would cover up.

"Now we both know that you aren't shy. Speak your mind."

He's referring to me taking off my bathing suit top. The way that he stares at me is like Superman using his x-ray vision. I had better take up the challenge. "I love camping. My family has been coming here for years. And what brings you here?"

"I actually live in Parry Sound, not far from here."

"All year round?" I ask.

He smiles. "Most people think that people only buy cottages around here. But my family likes to live in a neighbourhood with other Dutch people and enjoy nature all year round."

"I envy you," I say. "I always hate leaving here. It's so beautiful."

"I'm going to hate leaving here too," he says.

"Why leave?" I ask.

"I've joined the army."

"What? I mean why?" I stammer.

"Because I love Canada and I want to do something for my country."

"Wow. I never met anybody in the army before, except for old war veterans."

"I'm not a vet, just a cadet, taking officer training at RMC — that's the Royal Military College in Kingston."

"Do you like it?" I ask.

"It's hard work, but the army pays for my education. I couldn't afford to study science otherwise."

"Science! That is my best subject at school. I want to become a marine biologist. I'm fascinated with living organisms in the water."

"I specialize in space science. We have something in common. Astronauts train in water to mimic the anti-gravity movement that they will encounter in space."

"That's really cool," I say.

"What's not cool at RMC is waking up at the crack of dawn for marching drills."

"Yes, but it keeps you in great shape," I say, wistfully, missing the runner's high I used to get from feeling my feet pounding on the ground while jogging.

"That's true, but the really tough part will be when I have to go back for my summer survival training."

"That sounds intense," I say.

"It is. But after my undergrad, I'm going to apply for the Air Cadets because I love to fly. I've had my civilian flying licence since I was seventeen. I feel like a bird, free and wild when I'm up in the sky."

"That's how I feel when I kayak."

"Then you know what I'm talking about," he says. "We never had much money and I've always wanted to travel. Being with the army, I will have plenty of opportunity to travel."

"I've never met anybody so sure of the career direction that they want to go in," I say. Unlike myself, I really haven't thought about my career direction since the accident. I should tell him about it, but just as I am about to speak, the girls return.

"We brought you ice cream," says Karen. "Cherry cheesecake — your favourite."

Margriet hands her brother a chocolate swirl. Vanilla twisted with chocolate. Both cones are melting.

"What time did Papa say that we were playing miniature golf?" asks Margriet.

As Zef tips his hand to look at his watch, he plops his ice cream onto my lap. He looks horrified. He grabs my towel but stops when he realizes where the ice cream has landed.

"You better let me do it," I say, taking the towel from him and cleaning up the mess.

"I'm sorry," he says.

"No problem. You can share mine."

He bends down and takes a lick of mine.

We stare into each other's eyes.

"The time?" Margriet reminds Zef.

"Ah, yes, the time." He looks back at his watch and frowns. "I promised that I would drive them."

"Can Karen come too?" she asks.

"Of course," he says.

"Yes!" cries Karen.

As Zef stands up, he inadvertently kicks a shower of sand on me. "Sorry! Again!" he says, but I start to laugh and so does he. "What are you going to do now?" he asks.

"Take a shower," I answer and we both laugh again.

"Seriously, want to come?" he asks.

I glance at my wheelchair behind the tree. I don't want him to ever know. I cut my losses and say, "I have a boyfriend."

24

I TAKE A SHOWER. I WANTED A long shower, but the hot water runs out fast. I like Jamie and he likes me, but he still has feelings for Kat. I don't want to play tug of war for him. I tug at the tangles in my hair. And Zef will be leaving for his training soon. Which leaves me solo even before I'm a duo.

I dry off, change and sit at the campsite playing with the hot embers in the fire with a stick. Karen is off having fun playing miniature golf and my parents are enjoying a hike. And here I am, all by myself when who should come by but Jamie.

I light up. I'm relieved to have someone to talk to. "Hey, Jamie."

"Hey." He sits beside me in a camping chair. "I went mountain biking with the guys and we really tore up the dirt. There are some steep hills on the trail and great jumps. My bud, Bruno ran right into a tree. It was so funny."

"That's not funny." I sit up rigidly. "Was he hurt?" I ask.

"He's got a bump on his head the size of a golf ball, but, no big deal," he says.

"No big deal? Was he wearing a helmet?"

"No, but like I said, he's okay."

"Did he black out? He should be checked out at the hospital for a concussion," I say.

"Relax, Teresa. He's gonna be all right."

I'm seeing Jamie differently since I met Zef. Jamie now seems immature in comparison. He's also three years younger — which would explain part of it.

I like Jamie, a lot. He's a lot of fun, but Zef . . . he's different. He's serious and intense.

When Jamie makes a move to kiss me, I realize it's not fair to lead him on. I like him too much, so I quickly say, "I think it's a good idea if we . . . "

"Take it slow? No problem." He leans over and finishes his move.

Why do I smell Zef's pine aftershave when I'm kissing Jamie? The feeling of someone watching sends shivers down my back. I tear myself away from Jamie and look up.

Standing there is Zef!

25

"Who's the dude?" Jamie asks.

I look in panic from Jamie to Zef.

"I'm Zef, a friend. I can see that I've come at a bad time."

Jamie seems nonplussed. "Hey, no problem." He winks at me.

Zef winces.

To cover the awkward moment, I make small talk. "How was the miniature golf, Zef?"

"The girls enjoyed it."

"That was fast," I say.

"It's a small course." His answers are flat and curt.

"Where are they?" I ask.

"At my campsite."

Jamie looks confused.

"Our sisters are friends," I explain.

"Cool." Jamie stands up stretching. "I've gotta go. I promised to play touch football with the guys. You want to join in Zef?" he asks.

"No, not my game," says Zef.

"What is your game?" Jamie challenges.

Zef's face turns red. "I don't really do games," he says.

Yet Jamie is unfazed. "Well, glad to see that Teresa has a friend to talk to while I'm gone." He turns and leaves.

Zef just stands there staring at my wheelchair as if things couldn't get any worse. I forgot that this is the first time that he has seen it. Now he knows. "I'm surprised that you are still here," I say.

"I wasn't sure if you were using a line or if you really did have a boyfriend, so.... I can see that you were telling the truth."

"I do, I was . . . I mean I just met Jamie and we hang out together."

"Looks a little more serious," says Zef.

"You don't understand . . . " I stammer.

"You don't have to explain. I should go."

"It's not what it seemed . . . He kissed me. I wasn't . . . " It's pointless to go on. I start to cry. I never cry.

"Hey, it's okay." Zef sits down and hugs me. "Don't cry. I'm here for you. I'm not going to give up so easily because I really like you."

"What about my wheelchair?"

"What about it?" he says. "Were you always in one?"

"Car. Hit-and-run. I remember the exact day, place and time like it was yesterday. Almost a full year ago. Saturday, September 21, 10:33 AM at the corner of Bathurst and Eglinton in Toronto. The weather was foggy."

"Do you remember anything else?" He presses.

"No, not really. My therapist says that I have blocked it out because it was so traumatic."

He looks pensive staring into space.

"Earth to Zef," I say.

He refocuses. "Sorry, it's a lot to absorb. I'm sure this is painful to talk about," he says. "I admire the way you are so independent."

"Thanks." I unclench my hands.

"And you are so easy to talk to," says Zef.

"Are you trying to butter me up?"

"Just telling a beautiful woman the truth."

I'm swallowing his words, hook, line and sinker, and expecting him to kiss me.

Except Mom and Dad appear. "Hi, Mom, hi, Dad. Have a nice hike?"

"Ah, yes," says Mom. Dad is staring at Zef.

Zef moves away from me as if I have a contagious and fatal disease. He is all embarrassed. It's ridiculous. Every time I want to kiss a guy, my parents seem to magically appear.

He stammers away apologetically to my parents, promising to stop by in the morning, then leaves quickly.

The Kayak

Now I don't know if he wanted to kiss me as much as I wanted to kiss him.

That night, I dream of finding that deserted beach we passed in Bill's boat and sharing it with Zef.

When I wake up, I'm determined to turn my dream into reality.

26

THE NEXT DAY, I'M SITTING AT my campsite daydreaming about Zef when Jamie comes by.

"Hey," he says.

"Hey yourself," I answer.

My father sweats as he splits firewood and Jamie insists on finishing up the pile. Then he helps my mother put up the clothesline. My parents exchange looks. He's impressing them. And me. Now I'm really confused about my feelings for Zef and Jamie's feelings for Kat.

When he finishes helping, he comes over. "Want to go for a walk? I mean, I'll push?" he says half-flustered.

"Thanks for helping out, but . . . "

"Is anything wrong? asks Jamie.

I shrug.

"If it's about Kat . . . "

"I don't want to come between you and Kat."

"We're over for good this time. I only want you." Jamie looks at me with his big puppy-dog eyes. "Besides, you saved my life, so I'm obligated to save yours," teases Jamie.

"But I don't need saving," I say.

"Don't I know that? You are one strong lady." He looks at me with such tenderness.

I flex my biceps.

"Whoa. Look at those muscles. I'm not messing with you. Hold that pose." He snaps me flexing my muscles. He glances at his watch. "I promised Bruno that we would go biking. Do you want me to cancel?"

"No, go ahead, but make sure you both wear a helmet this time, okay?"

"Okay, Mom," he teases. "See you tonight?"

"I'm looking forward to it," I say.

Jamie walks away looking like the cat that ate the mouse.

As I think about Jamie and the evening, I hear an approaching plane.

Everyone on the beach turns around and watches. The seaplane makes a perfect landing on the lake and glides along the water, slowing down and eventually stopping near our beach. A man gets out, secures the plane, then dives into the water in his cut-off jeans swimming for shore. He looks familiar.

It's Zef.

"Zef!" I call.

He hears me and waves as he swims to shore. He climbs out of the water all sexy and dripping wet like James Bond. He walks right over to me.

"Hi, Teresa," he says, grinning.

Zef looks stunning and I must look stunned. "Hi," I manage to say.

"My buddy's father flies tourists around the area. And guess what?" he asks.

"What?"

"He cut me a deal renting a plane for the afternoon. Want to go for a ride?"

"You've got to be kidding?"

"I never kid," says Zef smiling. He scoops me into his arms. I don't want him to ever let me go, but he does. "You have to swim out to the plane."

"No problem," I say.

When we reach the floatplane, Zef gets out of the water, climbs into the plane and with a winch lowers a harness that is used to lift supplies. I put it on and he hoists me into the passenger seat. I unbuckle the harness while he unties us from the buoy. Then he hands me a headset.

"Better put this on. It can get noisy in here at full throttle." He shows me how. "Let's see Georgian Bay from a bird's eye view," he says. "Fasten your seatbelt."

I'm breathless as we take off. What promised to be a boring day has turned into the most perfect first date. Flying is exhilarating. We pass over one island after another.

Zef points. "That's our island."

"Our island?"

"Yeah, where we met. You were quite an eyeful, I recall. Nearly crashed my boat when I saw what I thought was a mermaid."

I punch him in the arm and he laughs.

"It's beautiful up here," I say. "You can see so far."

"You're beautiful," says Zef.

We don't say another word. I take in the wonderful sights, feeling breathless. *He thinks I'm beautiful.*

The plane starts to descend. "Time to take her down," says Zef.

We fly through the clouds and soon I can see our campground below us. Zef gently lowers us down. I gasp as we touch water and we glide. The plane slows down and comes to a complete stop. Zef opens up the door, climbs onto one of the pontoons and ties up to a buoy. He gets back into the plane while I put the harness back on and he lowers me onto the pontoon. He jumps, and I slip into the cool Georgian Bay water. All of my senses come alive.

"Race you to shore," says Zef.

"You're on," I say. And off we go.

I can just imagine the look on my parents' faces when they see me swimming away from the plane.

27

"Mom, Dad, Zef took me . . ."

Mom interrupts, "How could you take my daughter up in a plane?"

"Who gave you permission?" says my father angrily.

"Let me explain," says Zef.

"You better," says Dad.

"I'm a certified, experienced pilot and I'm in the Royal Military College. I should have asked your permission first. For that I am truly sorry."

That takes the wind out of my parents' sails.

"Well, I didn't know that you were certified," sputtered Dad.

"But are you sure that it was perfectly safe?" asks Mom.

"Yes, Ma'am."

"Well, then," says Dad. "Next time..."

"Next time?" squeaks Mom.

"We'll talk about this later, honey," says Dad as he leads her away.

"Whew," I sigh. "They can be difficult at times."

"I like that they are protective. You deserve it. Can I see you tomorrow?" asks Zef.

"You bet," I say. "But I'll make sure that I clear it with my parents first. I don't want you to have to go through that again."

"Neither do I," says Zef.

We sit silent for a moment.

"Do you want to go kayaking with me?" I ask.

"I don't know," he hesitates. "I was kind of hoping to take you out in my motorboat."

"I went up in your plane, so now it's time for me to call the shots," I say.

"Sounds only fair," he says. "I'll meet you on the beach tomorrow morning."

I'm still feeling elated long after Zef has left. Going up in the plane was a date like I've never had in my life.

Tomorrow I have to outdo him. I'm going to take him to that secluded beach that I saw from Bill's fishing boat. It's a far paddle, but Zef is in amazing shape. I wonder if he's ever kayaked before? I pull out a map of Georgian Bay and study it. We will be alone on a deserted beach. This is going to be so romantic!

That evening, I'm not excited about going out with Jamie. I mean, how can I expect him to top my date flying with Zef? I know it's not fair to think that way, but I can't help it. But I don't want to break my date with him because he can be sweet and sincere. Besides, there's nothing to do at my campground, but play cards and I'm really not in the mood.

Finally, Jamie comes to pick me up. "Hey." He kisses me briefly on the lips.

"What do you want to do?" I ask.

"Are you kidding me?" he teases.

"Besides that." My eyes dart over to where my parents and Karen are sitting by the fire.

"The guys are all going cliff diving, but I can just watch with you if you like." He doesn't look very happy.

"No, don't be silly. It will be fun watching you jump," I say.

"Really?" He lights up.

"Really," I say, meaning it.

"Okay, let's go." He starts to push me.

"Jamie?"

"Yes, Teresa," his voice is soft and sexy.

"Just be careful," I warn.

28

I watch as Jamie, Mario, Bruno, and others whose names I don't know, climb higher up the granite rocks. They stand on ledges of a small cliff and get ready to jump into the water. Some of the girls jump off the lower rocks, screaming all the way down. A couple of the guys do it too, but add cannonballs, making a great big splash and crying, "Cowabunga" all the way down. Others have ventured midway and jump from there, but Jamie climbs higher and Mario climbs with him. They go to the very top.

Jamie's on the ledge taking pictures of the cliff jumpers. I shield my eyes from the sun. I'm nervous. Doesn't Jamie realize the danger? Does he want to end up like me? If he doesn't clear the rocks, he's going to break his neck. Mario takes a run. *Come on, Pasquali jump far out*, I pray. He barely clears the rock jutting out and lands feet first into the water. He surfaces with a yelp and fist in the air. Stupid idiot. Now it's Jamie's turn. He hands his camera to one of his buddies. I don't want to look, but of course I do. I hold my breath as he runs. But he stops suddenly and teeters at the edge. The wind has picked up and the trees bend. Jamie will be jumping against the wind. That means that he needs to jump further out. The guys below are egging him on, "Jump, jump, jump!"

"Don't do it," I shout. Jamie doesn't hear me or chooses to ignore me.

He goes back, runs, and leaps. He doesn't make a sound as he plunges downward.

He splashes feet first into the water and bursts to the surface, arm in the air hooting. When he climbs out everyone is all over him, congratulating him.

Kat walks by me. "Hi, Teresa, I'm hot and can't wait to get into the water. Want to jump, I mean, watch me jump off the cliff?" she asks.

The air is humid and I'm sweating like crazy. "Do you want to go for a swim instead?" I ask.

"No, too boring — no offence," she says.

Whenever someone says 'no offence,' they usually say something offensive. I decide to go swimming without her. "Will you put my chair under the tree after I get in the water?" I ask.

"Sure," Kat says.

I wheel myself to the water's edge and slide down into the cool water. "Ah," it feels so good.

Kat takes care of my wheelchair and then starts to climb to the lower ledge. I watch the look of excitement cross her face as she jumps. She plunges feet first into the water and screams with triumph when she resurfaces. I envy her. I wish that I could do that too. She climbs a little higher, but chickens out and goes back to the lower ledge. She yells, "here I come ready or not," and jumps. I applaud and she lifts her arm in triumph looking at me smiling and climbs and jumps again.

Jamie climbs to the highest ledge. *Once, lucky, twice the fool?* I wish that he would call it quits.

I hear kids prodding a boy named Donald to climb higher. "Go Donald, go Donald, go, go, go," the crowd yells. He is a chubby guy. Someone yells, "Where's your bra?" Others laugh. Donald keeps climbing, but he has to stop to catch his breath. The taunts continue until he makes it to the top. He climbs out on the ledge and looks down. He is frozen. Other kids yell, "Don't be a wimp. Make it happen." He changes his mind and climbs back down. The other kids laugh at him. I feel sorry for him.

One kid sings, "Blood on the saddle, blood on the ground, great big blobs of blood all around."

Everybody joins in. "Second verse, same as the first, a little bit louder and a little bit worse." Then they belt out the lyrics.

Jamie is again at the top of the cliff. He runs and stops, teetering at the edge. Below, a motorboat floats too near his landing area. "Move," he cries waving at the boat.

The driver of the motorboat moves further out to watch.

Jamie takes a run. Did he jump too early? I can't watch. I tread water and look away.

I hear a yelp as he surfaces. "Wahoo!" I turn to watch him disappear beneath the waves again.

"What the . . . " Then I catch a mouthful of water as Jamie pulls me under. I come up sputtering for air. "You caught me by surprise." I splash him and he playfully splashes me back.

Jamie races me back to shore and helps me get back into my wheelchair. He spreads out his blanket, and assists me onto it. Then he finds a pail and bucket that some kid left on the beach and we build a sandcastle together. Bruno walks over. "Here's your camera, bro."

"Thanks. Go for another jump and I'll take your picture."

"Okay."

We watch Bruno climb and ham it up as he jumps, by pounding on his chest like an ape all the way down.

"I got some good shots," says Jamie. He shows me pictures of his friends jumping.

"Let me see more," I say.

"Here's you on the horse and me tipping your kayak, and my all-time favourite, you sprawled out in the mud."

"That's blackmail material." I smile. "You know you are good, really good."

"Thanks. I like taking candid shots."

He puts his camera safely away in its case, then casually adds, "You still seeing that friend of yours?"

"You mean Zef?" I ask.

"Yeah, him."

"Why?" I ask.

"He gives me the creeps."

Jamie is just acting jealous, but I feel torn. Jamie is so much fun. Zef is older and serious, but he's kind and gentle. After the accident, I thought that I would never have a boyfriend, and now I have two. It's much too complicated.

That night, I have a nightmare. I'm jogging then bam! I feel pain, confusion, fear and anger. Then it's as though I've left my body and I'm watching from above as a young man in a blue, beat-up Ford truck stops, stands over me, gets back in his vehicle and leaves me there alone lying in the middle of the road.

I wake up sweating. I never remembered so much about the accident before. I only remembered being hit from behind and lying on the road. Then nothing. Later, the police told me that a middle-aged woman found me and called an ambulance. I try to picture what the man in the truck looked like, but it's all a blur.

Was my bad dream allowing me access to my subconscious? Was that real or fabricated information that I pieced together? Was my mind playing tricks with me? Or did the trauma of the accident cause me to have an out-of-body experience?

29

THE NEXT MORNING WHEN I WAKE up, I remember that today is my outing with Zef. I hurry to get ready. I make a picnic lunch to take with us and pack the food into a dry sack.

Zef meets me at the beach. "Good morning," I say.

"It's going to be a great day today," says Zef as he looks up at the sky.

"Yeah, it's going to be a great day," I echo, meaning something totally different as I think of us on our own deserted beach.

Zef helps unlock the kayaks and put our gear into their hatches. He carries the boats to the water's edge. We put on our skirts and life jackets. I'm expecting him to do a hula dance or something crazy like Jamie did, horsing around, but Zef's too sophisticated to act silly. I wish he would loosen up a little.

"Do you know how to kayak?" I ask.

"I've been in all kinds of boats since I was four. I usually canoe, but I've kayaked before."

"Good, because I was hoping that we could go for a long paddle. I found a gorgeous beach for a picnic." I don't say 'secluded' because I want to surprise him.

"Sounds like a plan."

"But you still have to do the knock-knock test to make sure that if you tip that you don't panic," I say.

"I don't need to," says Zef. "I've done many manoeuvres in the water with canoes, kayaks, and rafts."

"It's my kayak. So prove it," I insist.

"Fine. What do I do?" He sounds impatient.

I explain the knock-knock test.

Zef takes the kayak out and flips it upside down. His arm shoots out of the water and his hand knocks three times on the upturned boat before he resurfaces.

"Good."

He looks annoyed as he swims the boat to shore and empties it of water. "That was a waste of time and now I'm all wet."

This is a side of Zef I hadn't seen before and now I'm having second thoughts about spending the day with him.

Zef helps me into my kayak and then grabs his paddle and gets into Karen's kayak. We start paddling.

What Zef lacks in technique he makes up for with sheer strength. He has no trouble keeping up with me.

The Kayak

I'm tired of kayaking in silence. This is supposed to be fun. "Zef do you know any knock, knock jokes?" I ask.

"They're childish. "

I sigh. "Do you want to sing?"

"Not really," he says.

This isn't going as planned. I'm half tempted to stop at the next beach, crowded or not. I think of how much more fun this outing would be with Jamie and his joking nature. "Do you want to stop?" I ask.

"I don't care," says Zef.

"Fine, then we'll stop here." The beach is small and part of the mainland. We just passed a couple of the nicer looking beaches and this one is small with gravel but I'm so turned off at this point anything will do. I don't see anyone here as we land.

Zef carries me out and places me on a dry flat rock near some juniper bushes, interspersed with blueberry bushes. "Hey, blueberries." They are on low-growing bushes and I pick and eat them. They are sweet and juicy. "Mmm." I smack my lips.

I hand him some blueberries. "Try these," I say.

He pops them into his mouth and makes a sour face.

I laugh. "I guess you got an unripe one."

"Stick out your tongue," he says. I do. "It's blue," he laughs. I'm relieved that Zef is finally lightening up.

He points to rabbit droppings. My eyes follow them and then I point in delight. "Look, a rabbit is hiding next to that rock covered in moss. Isn't it cute?"

"I wish I had my gun with me," he says.

"What?" I say, shocked.

"I like to hunt. I can just taste the great stew that rabbit would make. "

"I'm vegetarian. How could you kill that cute bunny?"

"You wear leather don't you?" he asks.

"Yeah, so?"

"Animals are killed so that you can wear leather shoes and belts."

"That's different," I say.

"No, it's not."

I can argue with him, but there is no point. I'm feeling uneasy.

Zef takes my hand. "Hey, I'm sorry, I was being insensitive."

"That's okay," I say. My stomach unclenches and then growls. We both laugh.

"I'm hungry too." Zef carries over the knapsack containing our picnic lunch.

He sits down beside me. "You are very special. I like being with you."

It's weird. Zef is like Jekyll and Hyde. One minute he makes me feel uncomfortable and the next, he makes me melt. As we sit side by side, I can feel the chemistry sizzling between us. I'm waiting for Zef to make a move and kiss me. He doesn't. So I take the initiative. I lean over and kiss him. He jumps away.

He composes himself. "Teresa, I'm flattered. But I'm too old for you. I enjoy your company . . . he pauses studying my face, 'as a friend.'"

I watch a crayfish burying itself in the sand. I wish that I could do that. I want to run away, but I can't. I look down. "I'm really embarrassed," I say.

"Don't be. I'm sorry if I led you on," he says.

"I'm so stupid. A guy like you must have lots of girlfriends," I say.

"I wouldn't say lots," his eyes twinkle. "I've had girlfriends of course, but I've been too busy studying and then training for the RMC to have any serious relationship."

I start to cry and he pulls me close.

"You are a very beautiful and smart woman. Of course, I'm attracted to you."

"You are?" I'm lost in his dark eyes. "You're only three years older than me."

"Right now you are almost jail bait, but I'm willing to hang around and be your friend. In a few years, if you still like me, we can take our relationship to the next level."

"I'll wait," I whisper.

"You say that now, but you are going to meet guys your own age and well, I can't ask you to wait for me," he says. "Friends?"

My eyes open wide.

Zef turns to look. "What the . . . "

A black bear with its baby comes out of the woods.

I open my mouth to scream, but nothing comes out.

30

THE MOTHER BEAR GRABS OUR KNAPSACK and starts dragging it away.

"Get," he yells. The baby bear takes off into the forest, but Mama bear faces us. She has huge sharp teeth and claws. Zef throws sticks and stones in the direction of Mama bear to scare it away. He yells at the same time. He grabs a stick and holds it over its head. Bears having terrible eyesight and that makes Zef look huge in her eyes. Mama bear drops the knapsack with our food and backs away. Zef keeps moving forward making noise and throwing stones with his free hand until she runs off into the woods.

We are both so busy watching Mama bear that we completely forget about baby bear. "Zef," I cry. But it's too late. Junior grabs the knapsack before Zef can get back and runs off with our food into the woods at full speed.

Zef and I look at each other in disbelief. Then we start to laugh. I'm laughing so hard that tears run down my face.

"Wait until I tell my buddies in the RMC. Great manoeuvre strategy. Mama is the diversion while Junior carries out the operation."

"That baby bear was big," I say.

"He was probably a yearling."

"Outsmarted by a bear," I say, wiping the tears from my face.

"Outsmarted by a team of bears," Zef corrects me.

My stomach rumbles. "And I made tuna fish sandwiches and couscous salad, with pickles for us."

"Stop, you're killing me. I'm starving."

"I can't believe I took tuna sandwiches into the wild. The bears must have smelled the fish from kilometres away. Of course it didn't help that we stopped in an area covered in blueberry bushes." I shake my head. "I have a granola bar in my kayak that we can share," I say.

"It will have to do." Zef holds his growling stomach. "We better head back."

Zef helps me into my kayak and I split the granola bar in half. We eat it slowly making it last.

We move out and have an easy paddle with the wind on our backs. When we land, Zef offers to take me out for lunch. He portages our kayaks and locks them up.

"I have dry clothes in my truck. I'll change in the men's washroom and meet you at your tent," he says.

Nobody is at my campsite. I think Mom mentioned something about going on a hike. I change and wait for Zef to pick me up.

He pulls up in a forest-green Ford truck. Dad's car is in front of our site and there isn't a lot of room for Zef to park. As he backs in, a tree limb scratches the side of his truck.

Zef gets out swearing and examines the damage.

I come closer to see how bad it is.

"Sorry I swore," he says. "I can use touch-up paint to fix the scratch."

"I see your truck used to be blue."

Zef shrugs. "Needed a paint job." Then he helps me into the passenger seat and puts my wheelchair in the back of the truck. We drive in silence to the diner. I can't shake the bad feeling I have, but then a deer appears at the roadside. "Look, a deer." I point. "It's so beautiful and graceful." Seeing the deer makes me happy. I glance at Zef but he stares expressionless at the road as he drives.

We reach the diner and it's not busy so we get served very quickly.

"This is the best grilled-cheese sandwich ever," I say.

"Or maybe it's your hunger speaking," says Zef.

Zef digs into his rainbow trout. It grosses me out because the fish head stares up at me.

There is a dartboard in the restaurant. "Do you want to play darts," I ask.

"Sure," he says.

I throw a dart; it hits the board and falls off.

Zef throws. "Bulls eye," I yell.

It's my turn. I throw and get the edge of the board.

Zef throws. "Another bulls eye. Wow. How did you get so good at this?" I ask.

"Practice," he says.

"I don't ever want to get on your bad side."

He turns to me. "I want to protect you. I don't want anything bad to happen to you."

I sit tall. "I don't need protecting. I can look after myself."

"Teresa. Disabled people are easy targets."

Jamie understands that I don't need protecting; why can't Zef?

Zef feels my unease and does an about face. "And I love kayaking with you," he says. "You have amazing stamina. You tire a man out," he says.

I've had so much tension today, nervous laughter bubbles out of me.

"What's so funny?" he asks.

"My date matched your date and trumped it," I say.

"Who would have thought?" He smiles.

"What we will do on our next date?" I challenge.

31

I FEEL LIKE I'M ON AN EMOTIONAL roller-coaster ride with Zef.

When we get back, Margriet runs to ask her parents if we can all come over for dinner.

My parents are only too happy to meet Zef's parents and spend the evening with them because they can keep a watch on us and size him up.

"Is that okay, Zef?" I ask.

"You realize that we will be under a microscope," says Zef.

I can't tell if he's teasing me or really feels under pressure. "You've met my parents, so it's only fair that I meet yours."

"Fair is fair," he says."

"See you tonight."

Zef is exhilarating and exhausting. I go back to the tent to lie down and take a nap.

In the evening when we arrive at Zef's campsite, Margriet and Karen hug each other and are off in their own world. Zef introduces us to his mother, father, and grandmother. They have thick Dutch accents, which surprises me because Zef and Margriet have none.

Mom brings over a bean salad which Zef's mother graciously accepts, placing it beside the other food on the picnic table.

"My goodness isn't this wonderful," says my mother. "Is that coleslaw?"

His mother says, "We call that Koolsla. Zef told me that Teresa is vegetarian so everything I made is Dutch vegetarian recipes."

"Thank you," I say.

She smiles at me. "You are welcome."

"What is this?" My father asks warily.

"It's a stew called stamppot. It is mashed potatoes mixed with mashed up vegetables. Start with the pea soup."

We dig in. Even Dad likes it. Typically, the men talk about fishing and the women exchange recipes.

Karen and Margriet eat quickly and disappear into the tent to do girl talk.

I try to act interested in the conversations, but I'm really watching Zef take care of his grandmother who is in a wheelchair. Maybe that's why Zef is not frightened of my wheelchair and is so accepting of me. I noticed that he filled his grandmother's plate before he sat down to eat. Zef is so attentive to his grandmother it warms my heart.

"Everything is so good," I say.

His mother looks pleased.

"I heard that Zef took you flying," says his grandmother.

"Yes. I loved it. I'm thinking that maybe one day, I'd like to get my pilot's licence."

"No kidding?" Zef looks excited.

"It's just a thought," I say.

My parents, on the other hand, do not look pleased. It will take some serious convincing, but there's no rush.

The two Dads make a fire and we sit around it eating dessert. Dessert is yoghurt with sugar and Edam cheese.

I help myself and eat. I hold my tummy. "I feel like it's going to burst," I say.

Soon, Karen is yawning and so am I, but I don't want this day to end.

His grandmother calls Zef over. "I am cold, will you get me my blanket?"

"Of course, Oma." Zef comes back with a quilted blanket that looks extremely familiar.

"Thank you, Jozef." She sees me staring open-mouthed at her blanket. "I made this blanket myself. Do you like it?"

I nod my head yes.

"I have made many blankets like this," she says, then stifles a huge yawn.

Dad takes this as a cue to leave. "Thank you for having us. I think it's time for us to call it a night."

"Can Zef walk me back?" I ask.

"Okay," says Dad heading for the shortcut.

Zef and I take the long way just to have some time together.

"Your parents are nice. Do you think they like me?" I ask.

"What's there not to like?

"I'm far from perfect," I say,

"Don't change anything," he says softly. "I like you just the way you are."

I don't want him to leave, but we've arrived at our campsite. "See you tomorrow morning?" I whisper.

Zef can't look me in the eye. "Teresa?"

"Yes?"

"I need to . . . " he clears his throat. "I need to tell you something." He sounds distant.

I wait but he doesn't say anything. "Zef, you can talk to me."

"It's nothing. I've just got a lot on my mind." He suddenly leans over and kisses me softly on the forehead then walks away, without looking back.

The Kayak

I am feeling unsettled. Zef does that to me. The stars are bright and the moon is full. I watch a falling star and make a wish. *I wish that Zef would trust me enough to tell me what's bothering him.*

32

ZEF DOESN'T SHOW UP THE NEXT morning, but Margriet does.

"I have a message from my brother for you," she says.

He sent his sister to deliver the "sorry I'm busy" message? If he doesn't want to see me again then let him have the guts to tell me himself.

"Zef was called in for summer training," says Margriet.

It's like a cold bucket of water is thrown on me. Why didn't he tell me last night? I never had a chance to say goodbye. I'm shivering and it's warm outside. "For how long?"

"Don't know."

"Where is he stationed?"

Margriet shrugs. "I don't know." Then she runs off. I'm left there stunned.

There's a lot I don't know about Zef. I don't know anything about his day-to-day routine in the RMC or what his life was like before he entered into the military. The list is endless.

But he never asked much about me either. He doesn't know anything about me before the accident. We hardly know anything about each other. We were both caught up in the moment. I spend the afternoon reading, or trying to read but I can't concentrate.

"What's wrong, Teresa?" asks Mom.

"What do you mean?" I put down my book.

"You seem distracted and out of sorts."

I have to tell someone or I'll explode. "It's Zef."

"What happened? Did you have a fight? "

"No, nothing like that."

"Then what?"

"Zef left," I say fighting back the tears.

"Oh, Teresa, I'm so sorry." She hugs me. "But, isn't he too old for you anyway?"

"We're just friends. Can't a guy and girl be friends?"

"Teresa. I didn't mean any harm. I just thought that maybe it's for the best. Now you can be with kids your own age, like Jamie."

"Kids, that's just it. Zef is a man, not a kid. He's only three years older than me. He's mature and understands me. Why can't you?"

"I'm trying, Teresa, but I can't when you get all worked up," says Mom.

"I'm upset because my friend just left without saying goodbye."

"I know that you like him, but . . . "

I take a big breath. There's no point in arguing. From the minute that I met Zef, we connected. He turned this holiday from good to great. I just wish that I had more time to get to know him better.

"Mom?"

"Yes?"

"Sorry, I yelled. It was a shock to learn that he left, that's all."

"I understand, honey."

"I'd like to go back to our campsite if you don't mind."

"No, I don't mind," she says.

I hear whoops of laughter as I leave the beach. I don't want to see anybody right now. "I'll help with supper, okay?"

Mom raises her eyebrows. "If you like."

Anything to keep busy. Anything to keep from thinking about Zef. When will I see him again?

33

Days go by and I can't stop thinking of Zef.

I decide that it's time that I forget about guys and go out kayaking. That's why we came to Georgian Bay in the first place. The waves are big and challenging and there are so many islands and waterways to explore.

I remember the map that Kat's father showed me. There was the secluded beach that I never had a chance to explore.

Karen is off horseback riding and I'm bored out of my tree. If I don't do something soon, I'll explode.

My parents help me launch and away I go. I have water and a snack. I pass Cousin Island, the Indian burial island. It feels haunted whenever I near it. It's an eerie feeling that I can't explain. It seems too holy to land. A raven stands guard on a tall white pine.

I'm going with the waves, which is wild and crazy. The kayak is lifted onto the crest then crashes down. I'm going so fast that I hardly have to paddle, only steer. I pass an island covered with dead trees, probably bug infested. I call it Dead Hollow. My theory is proven right when I see a redheaded woodpecker hammering at a hollow tree looking for bugs, and a squirrel dashing to a hole in the tree trunk.

The waves hit me sideways. It's tricky. If I lose concentration for one second the kayak will tip. Am I going too far? Should I turn back?

It didn't seem so far by motorboat. I should have reached the island by now. I have to pee so I need a beach. Any beach will do. And I'm going to land no matter what.

I'm not going to be stranded on an island like last time. I need to be more careful. I circle an island and pass a beaver's dam. Besides man, the beaver changes the environment more than any other animal. They can change a running river into a marsh.

I find a quiet corner, away from the wind and waves and stop at a small sandy beach. I face my kayak parallel to the waves, tip sideways and wriggle out in the shallow water. I quickly right the kayak so that only a little water gets in. I pull it out of the water, hauling it with the painter. From the side, I flip it over to get the water out, then flip it back. Then I tie my boat to a sturdy low tree branch and lie on the sand catching my breath.

Pulling off my bottoms, I pee. Then, feeling much relieved, I yank them back on. Suddenly I begin to feel itchy everywhere. I'm breaking out in hives. I look around me. No three-leafed plants. Good, I don't have poison ivy blisters. But what? Then I remember passing the beaver damn. I was in the water too close to the beavers and they can carry parasites that cause swimmer's itch. Great, just great. I stare at the raised, small bubbles all over my body. I then will myself not to scratch them.

I immediately crawl back into my kayak. Forget about finding my perfect island, I'm heading back. I paddle fast and furious, itching like crazy.

As soon as I get back, my mother takes one look at me and runs for the calamine lotion. Soon my body is covered in white guck. It helps a little and just as I begin resting on the beach, Kat shows up.

As she gets closer, she stares at my blotchy legs and arms. "What happened to you?"

"Swimmer's itch," I say. "What happened to you?" I ask. It looks as though she's been crying.

"As if you didn't know. Jamie dumped me. You must be happy," Kat says.

"I'm sorry that you were hurt. But we're all going home soon and I live far from Jamie. Who knows if I will ever see him again. Summer love never lasts."

Kat sits down in the sand. "I wanted the memory of this summer to be perfect, if you know what I mean."

"Yeah, I know what you mean," I say. *Summer love never lasts*, I repeat in my head. Am I talking about Kat and Jamie, Jamie and me, or me and Zef? I wonder.

Kat pours her heart out to me and I listen. Somehow, I don't hate her anymore. It's funny that of all people, she picks me to confide in. Girl-to-girl talk is something that I miss the most, and of all people, I have Kat to thank for sharing and caring what I think.

"I'm sorry that I've been giving you a hard time," says Kat.

"You keep life interesting," I say.

"I'm leaving tonight anyway," she says. "My father has to get back to work."

"And I'm leaving tomorrow," I say. "The vacation went by too fast."

"It always does."

I never thought that I would be saying this in a million years, but I ask, "Can I have your e-mail address?"

Kat smiles and writes it out in the sand. "Will you remember it?"

"I've got it." I point to my head. "It's easy. What I'll remember most is the look on your face when you had to run beside my horse in shorts through the raspberry bushes."

We both smile.

"I remember the first time I saw you. It was raining and you were all covered in mud."

I smile. "Jamie pushed my wheelchair so hard that I went flying into the mud. I wanted to make a good impression on his friends."

The Kayak

"You sure did," says Kat.

This gets us going again. We go through a list of 'I remember', before Kat finally has to leave. Today is the most fun I've had with a girl in a long, long time.

At dinner, my mother gives me an antihistamine and it works like a charm. My blotches and the itching thankfully begin to disappear.

Later that night, I'm expecting Jamie to show and he does. Now what do I really want? I'm feeling guilty that Jamie broke up with Kat to be with me, when my heart is with Zef. My evening with Jamie is nothing like I expect.

34

"I broke up with Kat for good," says Jamie.

"You've broken up with her and gotten together with her so many times that I've lost track," I say.

Jamie's face turns red. "We have a long history together. I've known her since kindergarten."

"Old friends are special," I say.

"Thanks for understanding. But I want to be with you, just you," he says.

"Great timing. I'm leaving tomorrow."

"You are?" He looks devastated.

"Remember, I told you last week?"

"The time went by faster than I thought. Teresa, we can make our relationship work."

"How do I know that you won't go back to Kat the minute I'm gone."

"Do I detect a little bit of jealousy?" teases Jamie. "Like I said, I'm over her and I'm over–the-top crazy about you. Okay?"

"Okay." He leans over and kisses me. He is a better than great kisser. When he stops, I'm light-headed. "How are we going to make this work? Jamie, you live in Ottawa and I live in Toronto. As you can see, I don't drive," I say.

"I can take the train to see you."

"I would like that," I say. We exchange e-mail addresses.

Jamie looks relieved. "You have a lot of guts and courage, that's what I like about you," he says. "And you are my guardian angel."

"If I was truly your guardian angel, I would be working fulltime to keep you safe because you are such a daredevil," I tease.

He takes my hand. "The gang is playing soccer in the field, would you like to watch?"

"Sounds like fun." I smile.

The sun is going down and I sit on the sidelines cheering Jamie on. He shows off by doing a back flip. I sit and joke with the other girls watching. It's strange not having Kat here.

Jamie's team wins and after the game, Jamie joins me all sweaty and talking fast about each great play his team made. It starts to drizzle.

We stop at my tent. It smells of wet pine needles.

"Want to go to the campfire tonight? he asks.

"Sure."

"I'll pick you up at nine." An ember flickers in the wet fireplace, catching our eyes. Sparks rise up into the sky. Jamie takes my hand. "One other thing."

"Yes?"

"Bring the marshmallows."

And the magic is back.

35

As I PACK, MY MIND WANDERS. Our last night together, was special. What happened? Nothing really. Jamie and I just hung out with the gang and held hands. Now that Kat had gone home, things were more relaxed between me and the other girls. Someone brought a guitar and we sang songs and roasted marshmallows. Maybe it was lame, but it was fun with Jamie by my side.

I have marshmallow all over my chin.

Snap.

"Jamie! I look awful."

"I think you look beautiful," says Jamie with a sparkle in his eye. "I'm going to miss you, Teresa."

"No you're not. How can you miss me when you have so many pictures of me?" I tease.

"I can never have enough pictures of you. Just one more." *Snap.*

"Jamie." I throw a marshmallow at him.

I can't believe our summer vacation is over. The time just flew. My holiday was certainly different than I had anticipated. Who would have thought that I would have one guy interested in me, never mind two?

Striking camp always takes much less time than putting up camp. I hear voices outside the tent and go out to see who is here.

Margriet is talking and hugging Karen. She says her goodbyes to us and then she hands me a letter.

"What's this?" I ask.

"It's from my brother. I'm glad that I didn't miss you because I promised him that I would deliver it. He also asked me to get your address."

I take the letter. Margriet hands me a piece of paper and pen and I write down my snail-mail and e-mail addresses.

"Call me, Karen," calls Margriet and she runs off.

I read my letter. He writes about the gruelling training he's been through, a bit about his buddies, the bad food, the rain, and the bugs. I skim through it fast, but stop, heart pounding and re-read the part about me.

"I've never met anyone like you. When I get a weekend pass from the RMC, I'll visit."

I put the letter into my chair pocket.

"What did he say?" asks Karen.

"He's going to try to get a weekend pass to visit."

"Tell him to bring Margriet," says Karen.

The Kayak

In no time, we are packed. We get in the car and head for home.

Sadness engulfs me as the trees become sparse and malls spring up like dandelions on the side of the highway. I leave Georgian Bay and my happiness behind.

The smell of car fumes and pollution from smoke stacks overwhelm me. The traffic is bumper to bumper and people honk their horns.

When we get home, I go to my room. It's nice having privacy again instead of being cramped in a small tent. I'm hot and sweaty. Mom turns on the air conditioning, but it doesn't refresh me like a jump into the cool waters of Georgian Bay.

I yearn to kayak and feel the wind in my face. Instead, I turn on the television and watch one rerun after another. Georgian Bay seems to be sliding from my memory like a dream.

Days tick by and each day seems the same.

I check my e-mail. My heart beats fast. Jamie has already e-mailed and he wants to chat with me on MSN.

"Hi, Jamie."

"Wassup?"

"Back home. Back to reality. And you?"

"Gotta work weekends at my Dad's pharmacy stocking shelves and doing deliveries. That means I can't come visit for awhile. $ is good. Miss u."

"Miss u 2."

"Pasquali's here to shoot some hoops. Talk soon."

"Say, hi from me. Bye." I sign off. Jamie is sweet and thoughtful.

I check my other e-mails. Nothing from Zef. Maybe he's too busy training. Or maybe he has already forgotten about me. I feel myself slipping into my old habits of TV, computer games and wearing my iPod. I'm busy doing nothing. Loneliness consumes me and I stare out the window like there are bars on them. Was I ever away? Why haven't I heard anything from Zef? I don't know whether I should be mad or sad.

Every so often, my mother comes in. As she talks to me, I listen from a distance. She brings in dinner. I take a bite and put it down. I'm just not hungry.

The phone rings. "It's for you, Teresa," calls Mom.

"Hello?" I say.

"Hi, it's coach Jim from the WBO. We haven't seen you for a while. We are short a player on the Viking team. Could I talk you into coming out again?"

He sounds so hopeful.

"I've never been good at basketball, not even when I could run," I say, trying to let him down easy.

"We just need a body. We can't play a proper game unless we have one more person on the team. We really need you."

When was the last time someone said to me that they really needed me? I hesitate. "Okay," I mutter.

The Kayak

"You won't be sorry. I'll see you at the Rec Centre at five."

"But . . . "

"Don't worry, you'll be great," and he hangs up.

"Great," I mutter to myself.

36

Dad is so excited. That's because he loves the game. As he drives me, he gives me a pep talk. "Being on a team gives you an instant group of friends, who are doing something fun together. You can, you know, be yourself with kids that are going through what you are going through."

When we get there, ten people in wheelchairs are shooting hoops.

"You the newbie?" asks a girl with a pierced eyebrow and black spiked hair.

"Kind of. I mean I was here a while ago, but I didn't last."

"I'm Spike, the captain of this amazing team. I guess you know Coach Jim standing by the hoop, the guy who called you, but well, he's got legs, so what does he know?"

I can't help but smile. "My name's Teresa."

"Welcome," says Spike.

Coach Jim comes over and shakes my hand. "Hi, Teresa, glad that you could make it. Let's see what you've got."

"Here, take a shot." Spike hands me a ball. I shoot and miss. Spike throws me another one. "Try again." I miss again. This goes on all through the warm up. I don't sink one shot.

"We just need an extra body on the court, so no pressure," says Coach Jim. "You'll get the hang of it." Coach goes over to talk to one of the other players.

Spike wheels up. "Hey, don't get down. You'll improve with practise. What are you good at?" she asks.

"Kayaking," I mutter.

"Only water here is in my water bottle. Let's see how you handle defence."

I shrug. "Why not."

The other girls join in and we start playing a game. I follow the ball around, but my teammates don't pass to me. I'm ready to throw in the towel when the ball is passed just over my head. My hands move in reflex and I surprise myself and my teammates by catching it. Three girls are coming at me, wheeling at full speed. I've got to do something fast.

One thing I am good at is survival and I weave in and out of players. Spike is open and I throw her a chest pass. She catches it and shoots. It circles the rim and goes in.

Spike screams and wheels over to give me a high five. "Smooth pass."

To my surprise, I'm smiling. Soon, the ball keeps being passed to me and I zigzag up the gym looking for someone on my team to be open. This girl with purple lipstick and matching fingernails is open and I pass to her. She shoots and yelps when it goes in. My team ends up winning. It's only a practice game, but I feel pumped.

Spike introduces me to everyone. Purple lips is called, Lynne. She has six-pack abs and large biceps.

"I know what you're thinking," jokes Lynne, "but no, I'm not on steroids." She does a fancy wheelie.

"How did you do that?" I ask.

Lynne shows me. "Go for it."

I do a pathetic imitation of a wheelie because I don't have the nerve to tip the chair back far enough, but to my embarrassment, I get applause from the team. I laugh. We all go out for pizza down the street. Some of the parents join us and sit at another table. I look over and Dad is really enjoying himself. It's the first time in a while that I've been hungry and I pig out on three pieces. Lynne packs away five. I can't keep up. By accident, I let out a burp and everyone acts like it's a badge of honour.

On the way home, Dad is more animated than I've seen in a long time. "You were so awesome. Some great passes! And the way that you weaved in and out, you moved so fast. Remember to always wait for the rebound.

And keep open. Cover your man . . . " I let him give me more pointers all the way home.

I actually look forward to my next practice.

I chat with Jamie. "Guess what?"I write.

"What?"

"I'm playing basketball."

"No way," he writes.

"Yes, way."

"What position?" he asks.

"Sitting," I joke.

"LOL," he writes.

"Small forward. I'm good at rebounds, steals and cuts to the basket."

"Go for it, girl."

"Did I tell you, I'm looking into university?"

"No. Where?" asks Jamie.

"First choice is Dalhousie in Halifax. They have the ocean in their backyard. Perfect for studying marine life. After the accident, I got behind in schoolwork. I need to hire a tutor to help me catch up and get better grades."

"You can do this, Teresa," writes Jamie.

"Thanks. I'm really excited."

"Gotta go to work. Talk tomorrow.

"See u." I turn off my computer.

Jamie e-mails me every day. I really look forward to it. It's nice that we have basketball in common. He sounds really excited about my games and always asks about every detail.

I know his schedule and eagerly turn on my computer and get on MSN hoping that he is connected.

"Hey, Jamie."

"Can I visit you?" He types.

"Yes!!!!!! When?"

"In two weeks, on your birthday, when you have your basketball tournament."

"You remembered." I'm touched.

"Of course I did. Or maybe I remembered from all the hints that you dropped."

"Very funny. I'm so excited."

"Great. Can't wait to shoot hoops with u. I can teach u a thing or 2," writes Jamie.

"Maybe, I can teach u a thing or 2," I write. But as I sign off smiling, I see that Kat is online, and re-sign on.

"Guess what?" I write.

"What?"

"My b'ball team's playing a tournament in 2 weekends, my 18th birthday."

"Your b-day! I'm coming in to celebrate and cheer you on."

"That's fantastic," I write.

"How's your team?"

"Not bad. We made it to the semi finals."

"Awesome. Guess what?"

"What?" I write.

"I have a new boyfriend, Dave. Really hot. Captain of the men's b'ball team."

"Need details," I write.

"Details to follow. LOL. I'll drive in with Dave."

"Jamie's visiting then too. Is that okay?"

"Totally. We're still good buds. I'll offer him a lift. Did I mention that Dave's really hot? See u soon."

We sign off. It's such a relief that we can all be friends.

Karen brings in the mail. She waves a letter in my face. "You got a letter. It's from Zef."

"Give it to me. " Karen holds it up high making me reach to snatch it from her.

"What's he say," she asks.

"Let me read it first."

I read, "*Sorry, it has been so long. I've been at summer camp. Ha ha. I mean, summer survival training camp. I'm stationed not far from RMC at Frontenac Provincial Park. Saw a black bear. Reminded me of the time we saw the bears and they outsmarted us. You would love how beautiful it is out here.*

"*I get a free weekend in two weeks and I'd love to drive down and spend some time with you. I have an old schoolmate named Todd who lives in Toronto. He couldn't hack it here. Too disciplined for him. I haven't seen him since last fall. I want to visit him too.*

"*See you soon!*

"Your friend, Zef."

Karen is hovering around me.

"He says that he is coming to visit in two weekends," I say.

"That's great, isn't it?" Karen studies my face.

"Jamie's coming then too."

"Both?" she asks.

"At the same time," I say.

37

Duration the following days, I'm busy practicing basketball, hanging out with my new friends, Spike and Lynne, and taking therapeutic horseback riding lessons.

Finally, my birthday arrives — along with two boyfriends in one weekend. This could be a disaster.

The doorbell rings. Is it Kat, Zef or Jamie?

It's Zef. He looks dashing in his uniform. "I'm sorry, I didn't stop to change."

My family is gathered all around us. I suddenly feel shy. I had been picturing a romantic kiss after our long time apart, but I just smile at him with everyone watching.

"Where are my manners," says Mom. "You can change in our bedroom." Mom shows him the way.

He re-appears wearing brown khaki pants and a tan shirt.

"You look nice," I say.

He bends down to whisper in my ear. "You look gorgeous."

I smile. "Thanks."

"I'm taking you out for dinner," says Zef.

"I'm so sorry, but that's impossible. I should have e-mailed you about my basketball tournament," I say. "We can grab a bite with the team after."

"Skip the game."

"I can't. It wouldn't be fair to the team, besides I want to play."

"I thought we were going to have some time alone together," says Zef. "There will be other games. I already made dinner reservations."

"We are in the semi-finals. The team will be disqualified if they don't have enough players on the court. I can't let them down."

"You are letting me down," says Zef.

This is not going well. Jamie and Kat are supposed to be here to watch me play. They're late. Now Zef's making me feel guilty.

"The team is waiting for me. We have to go. Are you coming?" I ask.

"I have no choice." Zef shoves his hands into his pocket.

Driving to the game, Zef doesn't say much.

Once I get to the Rec Centre, I try to forget about Zef, but it's hard. The player I am guarding has long red nails.

I call her 'Claws'. She's good at swivelling and weaving her wheels down the sidelines, so I have to work hard to block her.

"Ow." She scratches my arm, and draws blood. "You're not getting rid of me."

Claws trash talks me. "Hey, I saw you come in with that guy." She points at Zef. "Your boyfriend is more interested in his Blackberry than you."

I look and she's right, but know she's just trying to distract me. She now has the ball. I wheel fast; my arms burn, but I can't let up. I pass her, let go of my wheels, throw my arms up as she shoots, and just in time, deflect the ball.

"Your boyfriend is kissing the girl beside him," Claws taunts.

I refuse to look. "Yeah, right."

She ploughs right into me, sending me tumbling backwards. *Good thing I'm strapped in.* I push hard with my hands and upright myself.

The whistle blows, "Foul," cries the ref.

At the top of the key, I focus, take the shot, and miss. *I can do this.* I concentrate on the basket. My second foul shot drops. Yes!

The ref blows play in. I wheel hard. Spike passes to me and I dribble, then pass to Lynne who cuts to the right and swings hard to the hoop and sinks her layup.

My adrenalin is pumping. We have the lead with just 20 seconds to go.

The clock is ticking. The ball is passed to me. I try to slow the game down, so that we can hold onto the win. Claws claws me. Where's the ref when you need him? I fake a pass, but keep the ball, at the top of the key. Only ten seconds to go as Claws steals the ball and streaks down court. I have to stop her. She veers to the right and then bounce-passes to a trailing teammate. I lean sideways, crash to the ground, and get my hand out in time to deflect the ball.

Game!

I push myself up. My team is all over me, high fiving.

Lynne cries out, "Tomorrow we have the finals. We're just one win away from the championship."

Spike says, "I see that you were distracted during the game." She nods at Zef in the front row and winks at me.

I pretend to get the joke and force a smile. The truth is I'm disappointed in Zef. He didn't seem interested in the game.

Zef joins us. "Ready to go for dinner? I'm starved."

"Okay," I say, waiting for him to add something about the game, but he doesn't.

My teammates circle me and start singing "Happy Birthday."

"We are taking you out for Mexican burritos," says Spike. "Something hot and spicy."

I'm all smiles. "Thanks!"

Zef glowers at me. "Tell them we have other plans. Alone. I made reservations for the two of us."

"I can't let my friends down," I say.

"What about my plans?"

"Please? We won't stay long."

"You're calling the shots." Zef looks annoyed.

My friends joke around at the restaurant, but Zef doesn't try to join in. He sits there like a lump. If Jamie was here, he would have watched me play and then hang out with my friends. Where *are* Kat and Jamie? They missed the whole game. I get out my cell phone.

"Who are you calling?" asks Zef.

Embarrassed, I put it away. "Sorry."

He talks low to me. "You aren't like your teammates. They are immature."

No, they're not, I seethe.

"You've made an appearance, now it's my turn."

I'm not happy that Zef makes me leave early from my own birthday party. But I promised. "Okay, where do you want to go?" I force a smile.

"I just want to be alone with you."

We end up going to a coffee shop. Whoop-di-do! But I try to make the best of it.

"Did you see that amazing shot Lynne made from centre court?"

"I don't want to talk about basketball."

"Okay, what do you want to talk about?"

"I don't know." He shrugs.

"Movies? Did you see . . . ?"

Zef interrupts. "How could I see a movie when I was at survival camp?"

"So tell me about survival camp."

"I survived."

I get it; Zef is punishing me. I've had enough and pretend that I'm tired and start yawning.

"I'll take you home," says Zef.

During the ride, I turn on the radio so that we don't have to talk.

Zef changes my rock station to a country station.

Whatever. I'll be home soon and Zef can go stay in a hotel for all I care.

"You're back early," says Mom as she opens the door.

"I'm tired after the game," I say which is only partially true.

"Please, can we talk?"asks Zef.

Zef looks so disappointed that I have a change of heart.

"Okay." I shoo everyone out of the den and Zef and I sit on the couch. "How is boot camp?"

"Promise me we will never buy anything that you have to polish?"

Is Zef implying that he sees us married? I'm not ready to go there.

The Kayak

"My officer made me polish shoes, buttons, medals, trophies until they shined. At least he didn't make me brush his teeth." Zef relaxes talking about his life. "Thank goodness I got last weekend off and went home."

"You had free time? How come you didn't call or e-mail me? I haven't heard from you since your letter about visiting me. Here I thought you were in survival camp and couldn't get to a phone or a computer."

"I was busy helping my parents finish the basement. I didn't have time."

Of course I admire how he cares for his family, but he could have taken five minutes off to contact me.

"But I did have time to buy this."

Zef pulls out a small box and gets down on one knee.

38

I STARE AT ZEF DOWN ON ONE knee holding out the box containing a ring. *No, don't do this.*

He sees me wince. "It's not an engagement ring. It's a promise ring. I just want you to know that I mean what I say about waiting for you."

"Oh." But I don't feel any relief.

He slips the ruby ring on my finger. "It's your birth gem. I hope you like it."

"It's beautiful," I say and it truly is.

Zef is still on one knee. "I wanted this to be more romantic. That's why I made those reservations. I asked them for a table with candles and to play violins by our table. Now you know why I was put off when we had a change of plans."

"Zef, I can't accept this ring. Like you said, I'm too young to get serious. "

"I'm only asking you to be my girlfriend and not date anyone else." He puts the ring on my finger. "Please, don't say anything right now. Just think about it."

Right now, I need to break the tension between us. I need time to think. "Let me give you the grand tour," I say.

I show him all the ramps and renovations that my parents put into the house.

"I made ramps at our place for my grandmother. I also installed bars in the bathtub," says Zef.

I like that he is so considerate, plus that he is such a handyman. I ask if he wants to see upstairs, where my room is. He has to wait while I take the seat elevator up and transfer to the wheelchair upstairs.

Zef walks into my room and freezes.

"What's wrong?" I ask. "I know that it's a bit messy, but . . . "

He's looking at my shelf of trophies and medals.

Then he stops and stares at the quilted blanket draped across my chair. He touches it, tentatively.

"Oh, that. The quilt is a reminder that whoever hit me with the truck wasn't completely evil — just a coward. Even though they left me lying on the road to die, they covered me up with that blanket. After the police looked at it for evidence, I got it back. When I look at the quilt, I tell myself that one day the person who took my old life from me, will have to pay the consequences."

"Do you know anything else about the accident," he asks quietly.

"The police determined that it was a truck, I don't remember anything because I was hit from behind and knocked out."

Zef sits, as though some heavy weight has pushed him down. "I'm . . . I'm so sorry Teresa."

"For what?" I ask.

"For being so gullible."

39

"WHAT ARE TALKING ABOUT?" I ASK. I feel unnerved.

"Last fall, I came to Toronto to visit my best friend, Todd. He asked if he could borrow my truck to do a few errands while I caught up on my sleep. I gave him the keys.

"He came back looking a mess. I asked him what was wrong. He told me that it was so foggy out that he couldn't see his hand in front of his face. He hit something then veered into a tree. He said that when he got out to investigate, there was a dog lying bleeding on the road. He told me he covered it with the blanket — my grandmother's — that he found in the front seat and was on the way to the vet when the dog died. He left the blanket with it. He said he felt bad about wrecking my truck and later took it to a body shop to fix it and repaint it. He insisted on paying for it.

"I'm so sorry, Teresa."

"What does this have to do with me?"

"What you just told me about your hit-and-run, the date, location, time, and that it was foggy out . . . I believed Todd's story . . . until now."

"What do you mean?"

"When I saw my grandmother's blanket . . . Teresa? I'm sorry. I swear I didn't know."

I'm stunned. I can't think straight.

"Teresa, I swear, I'm going to make this right. First thing tomorrow morning, Todd and I are going to the police station and tell them what really happened."

Suddenly it's all clear and I find my voice. "You might be charged too, because it was your vehicle that hit me. And you will have to testify against your friend."

"I'll tell the truth. I didn't know. I'm a moral person. I have to do what is right to live with myself. I can't believe that my best friend lied and used me! And now, he'll probably go to jail. Which is nothing compared to what you've lost." Zef stares at my trophies and medals, then back at my wheelchair. "Please believe me."

"Yes," I whisper. "I believe you. You didn't know." Then I take his ring off my finger and hand it to him. "I can't wear this. I can't."

The colour drains from Zef's face. "I thought you said that you believed me?"

"I do believe you."

"Then what are saying?" Zef searches my face.

"It isn't about the accident. You're a good man, but it's not enough."

"What did I do wrong?" asks Zef.

"It's not what you did, it's who you are. We are at different stages of our lives. Like a baby needs to learn to crawl before it walks, I need to experience being a teen. I need to worry about what dress to wear to prom, have pyjama parties with pillow fights, and act silly. You're already an adult, worrying about your career and money. And now you have my accident to account for. We are going in different directions."

"I'll straighten everything out. I'll wait until you are ready," says Zef.

"No, I'm sorry I don't want you to do that."

"Forget the ring." He shoves it into his pocket. "Let's be boyfriend and girlfriend without it." He pleads.

"It's best that we not see each other."

Zef stares at me in disbelief. "Please . . . I love you."

These are words that I once desperately wanted to hear, but not anymore, not from him. We are worlds apart. "Please leave," I say quietly.

I wheel to the top of the stairs but do not watch as Zef goes down. There is a pause when he reaches the bottom. I imagine he is looking up. Then I hear the door open and close.

He is gone.

40

I'M NOT HALFWAY DOWN THE LIFT when the doorbell rings. Karen rushes to answer. In walks Jamie, Kat, and her new boyfriend, Dave. "Happy birthday!" they cry in unison and begin to sing, but stop when they sense the tension.

"I know you're mad because we missed your game," says Jamie.

"It's all my fault," says Kat rambling. "My car died and we had to wait for a tow truck and it turned out that I needed a new battery, so we had to wait at the garage while they installed it."

"That's not the problem," I say, trying not to cry.

"Teresa?" asks my mother, concern in her eyes.

I look at my family and my friends. "There's something I need to tell you."

The Kayak

It's a long night as I retell the events of Zef and me. There are tears, hugs, and a feeling of relief. I couldn't have done it without my friends and family.

In the morning, I actually feel as if a big burden has been lifted off me. I join my friends who are all sitting around the kitchen table having coffee. "I have the finals at 2:00 today."

"We missed your semi yesterday and we're not missing the final today," says Jamie.

Dave and Kat both click their coffee cups in agreement.

During warm-up my teammates keep passing to me just to see my friends go crazy every time I get the ball.

Jamie takes pictures the entire time.

Once the game begins, I focus on my defensive play.

It's like running a marathon, I get into the zone and forget about the outside world. With less than one minute left to play, we are winning by a single point. Spike and Lynne move down court, passing back and forth. Lynne shoots and sinks it. We have the lead by three points.

Coach calls a time out. "Play a full-court press to bottle them up. You can stop them."

I stay close to my opponent, like a second skin. They try desperately to dribble through us, for a last-second shot to tie. But Spike steals the ball, and the buzzer sounds.

Game!

My teammates are going nuts hugging one another. Coach congratulates us.

Jamie joins us on the floor and nearly gets run over. He's snapping pictures like crazy.

"Your defence was great," he cries to me.

"Thanks," I say, grinning.

Afterwards, Jamie shows off the pictures to me and my teammates. "You are really good," I say. "But maybe delete the one where I missed the foul shot and look stunned?"

"No way, that's my favourite," says Spike laughing.

Kat and Dave do a few set ups with some of the girls. Jamie borrows a wheelchair and goes one-on-one with me. We horse around and it is nice having Jamie on my level for a change.

"Ugh, this is harder than I thought," says Jamie.

"Suck it up," I say as I steal the ball, shoot and sink it.

Jamie gives me a high five.

After I say goodbye to my teammates, my friends and I go out to dinner. Jamie and Dave hit it off and talk so much that I roll my eyes.

Kat interrupts. "Remember me?"

Jamie shows us his pictures. We have a good time reminiscing about our summer vacation. "Oh, no, not the mud picture again," I groan.

"Let me see," says Kat grabbing at the camera. "There's me jumping from the cliff."

"What's this?" I ask, staring at a picture of a street person lying on the ground begging.

"Those are my pictures that I want to show my professor," says Jamie.

"Can I see them?" I ask.

"Sure."

I look at a picture of a doe's loving expression for its fawn; a photo of a fireman bravely carrying a child from a burning house; a shot of a policeman saving a cat from a tree while a child stares up at the officer like he's a hero; and a picture of bald kids in a hospital ward playing dress-up, laughing and forgetting for a moment that they have cancer.

My eyes tear up. "These are really moving, Jamie."

"Thanks," he says.

"How did you first become interested in photography?" Kat asks.

"My uncle Jack worked for *The Toronto Star* as their photographic editor. He taught me how each picture should tell a story. He inspired me. Just like you, Teresa."

I blush.

He scrolls through his pictures.

Dave jumps in. "Stop right there. I like this one of Kat doing a belly flop," he teases.

She sticks her tongue out at him.

It is good timing to be busy with friends. It helps me to forget. Kat and Jamie are old friends and have a history. Dave and I just look at each other, shrug and give each other a look that says something like, "Don't know what you two are talking about, but whatever makes you happy." Neither of us is jealous. The evening goes too fast and Kat and Dave have to leave first thing in the morning so we call it a night. Jamie's staying on and will take the train back home.

I give Kat a hug. "I want details," I whisper in her ear.

She smiles and we say our goodbyes.

The next morning, my parents surprise us. "We booked camping at Georgian Bay for a couple of days," says Mom.

"Thanks, Mom, I really miss kayaking."

"Jamie, we have a small pup tent, good for one person, that you can use to set up on our campsite," says Dad giving a little parental warning.

I go upstairs. There is one more thing that I have to do before we leave.

I pack Zef's grandmother's quilt to mail it back to her. Then I stuff my things into a bag and we all crowd into the van. We stop at the post office on the way.

We sing most of the ride up north to Georgian Bay.

The choppy waves rise and fall. I ride the crest of the wave. I smile over at Jamie and he smiles at me. Our kayaks bob like corks in the swirling waters of Georgian Bay. I love it. I feel alive and free. Out here, I am one with the kayak. The kayak is an extension of my legs. I can do anything; I can go anywhere. It is the same onshore; I am one with the water and with the land.

DEBBIE SPRING has been a published writer
since 1985. Her publication *Breathing Soccer*,
was short-listed for the 2010 Manitoba Young
Readers' Choice Award. Her short story, "The
Kayak", published in the anthology *Takes: Stories
for Young Adults* (Thistledown Press), was the
seed for this new novel. Spring lives in Thornhill,
Ontario.